RACE TO THE GREAT INVENTION

BRONWEN BUTTER NEWCOTT

F O X H A L L press
Foxhallpress.com

©2023 by Bronwen Butter Newcott

Cover design & illustrations: Marco Marella
Interior Design: Chris Sowers

Summary: 12-year-old neighbors Tessa and Gus are given a magical spyglass that shows them there is more than meets the eye. What begins as summer fun, turns into a wild adventure to save the people they love.

ISBN 979-8-218-20599-7

Printed in the United States of America

Library of Congress Cataloging in Publication Data
A catalog record for this book is available from the Library of Congress.

Close both eyes to see with the other eye.

-Rumi

CHAPTER 1

For the past half hour, Tessa and her neighbor Gus had been trying to rig up a hose-phone between the bedroom windows of their houses. They'd made a string-and-can phone before, but Gus figured they could simplify it. The plan was to stretch the hose above the alley between their two windows and talk through it.

Now it was a matter of swinging the hose Tessa was dangling out the window with enough momentum to reach Gus's window. They hadn't thought about the fact that the nozzle was metal and they were swinging it right above the living room windows until it slammed against the downstairs window frame, a near miss.

Tessa Hardy and Gus Tucker had lived next door to

each other for their entire lives and had gotten into their fair share of trouble. Last year they'd accidentally shattered Tessa's kitchen window playing baseball with a full coke can — a terrible idea all around — and had each needed to save $50 of allowance to go toward the repairs.

A hose-phone seemed safer. But it was proving to be harder to rig up than they'd expected.

"Not again!" called Tessa as the hose banged against the side of Gus's house for the eighteenth time.

Tessa, leaning halfway out the window but keeping her center of gravity, which she'd just learned about in her science magazine, below the sill, softly swung the thick green hose again and watched it arc nowhere near Gus's outstretched hands. She wasn't easily discouraged, but this was taking a long time, even for her. "I'm going to try five more times!" she called.

"Ok!" Gus called back, widening his stance to make himself more ready for the catch. Gus was the second tallest boy in the 6th grade, and everything about him was long and lanky. He had brown shaggy hair that turned almost gold in the summer, and his feet were huge. "Jackrabbit feet" is what his dad always called them. His parents said they'd been like that even when Gus was born. He reached out the window one more time as Tessa pulled the hose back and released it. This time it swung straight into his hands.

"Finally!" he yelled, pulling a length of the hose into his room.

"Let's try it!" Tessa called. Her mob of black curls bounced around her face as she did a victory dance. Her hair had been nearly to her elbow before she'd cut it last week to donate 10 inches. She couldn't believe how light her head still felt. Her sister's friends kept telling her that the short cut made her green eyes stand out. She'd always thought of them as muddy brown, but maybe they were kind of green?

Gus put his lips against the hose, stood to his full height, and hollered as loudly as he could. Tessa heard him mostly through the opened window and a spurt of cold water trickled down the side of her face.

"Ahhhhhhh!"

"What?" Gus called.

"We didn't drain the hose!" It was true. They'd turned it off, yes, unscrewed it from the spigot and let the water run out, yes, but they hadn't made sure all the coils were empty. Tessa laughed as she shook her wet head.

They yelled back and forth through the hose for a minute, which was really a lot like yelling through the opened windows, and then tried whispering. They could actually still hear each other.

"This might come in handy in a snowstorm," Tessa whispered, "or in the morning when it's too early to call."

"I know!" said Gus, getting louder so Tessa could hear him through the window again. "We could even send batteries through this thing if one of our flashlights dies in a power outage! Or —"

The end of the hose slipped from Tessa's hand and swung down between their houses.

"Or not," Gus said, and he let his end fall, too.

"RIP, hose-phone." Tessa called down to the green squiggle across the alley.

"It'll be ok," said Gus. "It was a good phone for a second. See you tomorrow!" he called, waving. "And don't sweat Samantha — it's almost summer!"

"Almost!" Tessa yelled back. Samantha Shaw. In all the years of elementary school, she and Samantha had never been *friends*, but they'd never been anything. Until this year, when the week before spring break Mary Murphy, the girl who sneezed ridiculously loudly during math tests, moved away, and Samantha needed a new target. For some reason, she'd picked Tessa, and Samantha got meaner every day. Tessa waved to

4

Gus and closed the window.

Instantly she felt the quiet of the house. An empty silent house felt a certain way, she'd decided. It felt like being watched from every direction and being completely alone at the exact same time. She didn't like it. Tessa stomped down the creaky wooden stairs, humming to herself. At least it was a Loochie day, and the house smelled of garlicky tomatoes.

Loochie — Tia Lucinda, formally — was Tessa's great aunt, a stout, grumpy, Costa Rican woman who loved Tessa's father but didn't care much for kids. After Tessa's mom had died three years ago, Loochie had insisted on helping out, so every week she came on Tuesdays and Thursdays during school to clean and cook dinner. Even though Loochie assaulted Tessa with complaints about her books on the floor and Tessa's not wearing dresses, Loochie days were the best because after she left, smells of dinner filled the house. Loochie, despite her nagging, was an amazing cook.

After her mom died, Tessa knew lots of parents thought she was too young to stay home alone after school, but Tessa's dad was different than most parents. He'd said she was "unusually capable and independent," and she'd felt so proud when he'd given her a house key of her very own.

But being independent was different than she'd imagined, especially this year. Molly, her oldest sister, had left for college in September, and Cassie, in 10th grade, had her driver's license now and always had somewhere to go. The house was mostly quiet.

Tessa took off her sneakers and kicked them into the middle of the living room onto the perfect vacuum tracks Loochie had left in the carpet. Then she rumpled the fluffed pillows so it looked like someone had been home and walked into the kitchen. The back door crashed open.

"Cassie!" Tessa shrieked, jumping.

Cassie smiled apologetically as she rushed through the room, her head cocked to one side, holding the phone between her ear and shoulder. Her long black hair swished behind her.

"I thought you had a softball team party?" Tessa called after her.

"Forgot the card we made Coach!" Cassie yelled back, running upstairs.

Cassie was nice enough, but she wasn't like Molly. The whole time their mom was sick, and even after that, Molly had let Tessa sleep in her bed and had met Tessa's school bus every afternoon. Tessa had tried to be happy for Molly when she'd gotten accepted to college in Rhode Island, but Tessa had felt her heart squeeze almost to death when Molly had left last September. Tessa missed her every day.

Tessa pulled out her phone and saw she had a text from her dad.

Home by 7:30!

She sighed. It was only 5:04. Her dad tried to be home by 7:00 every day, but as he often explained to Tessa, now that he'd been promoted, he was the "host" of the art museum, which meant lots of lectures, galas, dinners, and sometimes trips.

Cassie sped back downstairs. "LoveyoutellDadI'll-behomebynine!" She hurried out the door. "It's starting to rain!" she yelled, slamming the car door.

Tessa heard the engine start as rain began hitting the kitchen window. Maybe the storm would be big enough to knock the power out. Then they'd have to close the museum early and probably the pizza place so that Cassie would come home, too. They could all light candles and pretend they lived in Little House on the Prairie, like they used to do during storms with their mom when Tessa was little.

The lights flickered but stayed on.

CHAPTER 2

"I've gotta clean the garage windows," Tessa said, nodding toward the Windex. "It's the second-to-last day of school, but for some reason, my dad wants them washed today. Want to help?" She pulled a handful of candy from her pocket. "I brought Laffy Taffy."

"Bribery? I'm in." Gus grabbed the Windex. "But I'll need a steady supply of candy." Tessa grabbed another handful and held it out to him. "I'll get the top windows."

It was useful having a tall friend. Now Tessa wouldn't have to drag out the ladder. Tessa and Gus — August, really, but nobody ever called him that — had been friends for as long as they could remember. In fact, their parents were friends before they were even born, though they hadn't spent much time together since Tessa's mom had died and her dad had started working longer hours.

Tessa and Gus used to play at recess every day, building things out of dogwood berries and twigs, or acorns and oak seed propellers, depending on the season. For those forty minutes of freedom, they'd invented circuses, traveled through marshes by canoe, and spent a lot of time in space. But then, around third grade, the boys and girls kind of separated, and without even meaning to, Tessa and Gus stopped hanging out at school. Outside of school, though, they were still best friends.

"It's kind of funny that your dad even cares about this," Gus said, spraying blue Windex on the next square of glass. "It's not like the car needs a good view."

"That's as dumb as these jokes," Tessa groaned, unwrapping another piece of candy and reading aloud. "Ok, what did the buffalo say when he left for work?"

"I dunno, what?" Gus asked for the tenth time, spraying more Windex mist.

"Bison."

"These are the worst!" Gus said. "I love them."

"Last one." Tessa smoothed a yellow sticky wrapper. Gus had traded all his bananas for her grape. "Why do fish always sing off key?"

"Why?"

Tessa grinned. "Because you can't tuna fish!"

"Ha. Ha. Ha." Just then, a man with white wispy hair bustled past them down the alley muttering to himself.

"Professor Henchworth!" Tessa whispered loudly.

"Tessa!" Gus whipped around to make sure the professor hadn't heard her. "Not so loud!"

"But what do you think he's doing?" They watched the professor hurry down the alley, his white straight hair mussed by the wind. He had five long pipes hoisted over his shoulder. Each must have been about six feet long and were balanced precariously. Tessa saw the professor from time to time, and he always carried something odd — brown bags from the hardware store, pieces of wood, even shopping bags from the toy store, which was strange because he had no kids. Neither Tessa nor Gus had ever spoken to him, and it seemed to them that the professor was talking to himself as he walked.

"Is he on the phone?" Gus said.

"Nope — no air pods. I already checked. I wish we

could wiretap him and hear what he's saying," Tessa said as the professor turned the corner out of sight. "Do you think he's crazy, like certifiably insane?" The only things Tessa knew for sure about the professor were his name and that he lived in the only townhouse with a tall fence completely enclosing the backyard. But everyone in the neighborhood knew that, just like they knew the Chens lived in the grey corner house and Mrs. Merrill grew the wall of yellow roses.

"Maybe. Have you noticed he always wears the same thing?" Gus said.

"Brown?" Tessa guessed, trying to picture him in her mind.

"Yeah. The same brown jacket with elbow patches — even in summer — and he's always got two brand new pencils sticking out of the jacket pocket, eraser side up."

"How do you know that?" Tessa asked.

Gus shrugged. He noticed everything.

"I think he has a reptile farm in his backyard. And the stuff is for the feeders and cages," Tessa guessed.

"You only think that because *you* want a lizard," Gus said.

"A *horned* lizard," Tessa corrected him. She looked thoughtfully in the direction the professor had walked.

"This summer let's figure out what he's up to."

Gus's face brightened. "Challenge accepted!"

As they finished washing the windows, Gus tossed the last of the soggy paper towels in the trashcan. "Only two more days of school!" he said giving her a high five.

Tessa sighed. School couldn't end fast enough!

"You've got this," Gus insisted. "See you tomorrow on the bus."

CHAPTER 3

"**D**o I even need to ask?" Gus asked the next afternoon as he and Tessa kicked a rock back and forth between them down the alley.

"Nope." Tessa sent the rock skidding 20 feet ahead of him. She was tired of talking about Samantha. "But only one more day. Then three months without her!"

She and Gus were headed to the library to stock up on summer-reading books. Gus's mom, Mika, had persuaded them to go even though school wasn't officially over yet.

"Smell that?" Mika had asked. "When you get back, that chocolate cake will be out and frosted!"

"Fine, if we *have* to go," Tessa had said, exaggeratedly rolling her eyes. Mika had smiled at her. It was no secret that Tessa loved the library, and Mika's chocolate cake was good enough to motivate someone to scrub the porch with a toothbrush, anyway.

Tessa and Gus were walking down the alley instead of the sidewalk because it was Tuesday, the day before trash pick-up, the best day for trash-hunting. Narrow alleys ran through the neighborhood behind the rows of small garages and patch-yards. When anyone had junk to throw out, they propped it next to their big green garbage can to be hauled off. Once Gus had pushed Tessa almost a mile in an old desk chair they'd found. Another time they dragged home a broken computer, taken it apart with a screwdriver, and made a model house – a box, really – with the flat green circuit boards.

Gus picked up an old mesh wastebasket and put it on his head. He was pretending to fence with a cracked yardstick when an orange cat came over and wound itself between his legs, meowing loudly.

"Settle down!" he cried, petting the cat as it butted against his leg.

"Look!" Tessa said brightly, pointing to a blue chalk arrow on the ground, and another one about ten feet ahead. "It's a trail!"

"Maybe it'll lead us to a heap of trash-treasure!" Gus joked. He stepped over the cat who was still purring loudly and started walking in the direction of the arrows. Tessa almost had to jog to keep up with Gus's long strides. She wasn't *short* exactly, she'd just paused for a long intermission at 4'10". People kept telling her she'd have a growth spurt any day, but for now, she was holding fast. She didn't mind; she'd always liked her height.

The chalk arrows definitely made a path. Some were drawn on the pavement, some on bricks, and one was even on a concrete windowsill. The kids followed them around the corner, up the street, and through the neighborhood to the bottom of a hill where they finally seemed to drop off.

"Is that it?" Gus asked looking around.

"No!" Tessa protested. "There has to be another one!" As she scanned the bricks and concrete, Gus spotted a bramble of blackberry bushes beside a trashcan. He reached and pulled off the darkest ones, the fine thorns scraping his hands.

"Ouch!" He said, popping the berry in his mouth. "But mmmm, so worth it."

"I can't find anymore arrows," Tessa sighed.

"But who knew this bush was here? Open your mouth!" Gus said, aiming. A berry hit Tessa squarely on the forehead with a soft splatting sound and fell to the ground.

"Oops!" He laughed as Tessa wiped a smudge of purple juice off her face and tucked a loose curl behind her ear.

They picked berries until their fingers were stained and arms were covered in scratches. The cat, who still seemed obsessed with Gus, kept brushing against his leg and finally meowed loudly and ran off. The kids wandered after him. As they rounded a corner, the cat was nowhere to be seen, but Tessa instantly recognized where they were. Focused on the arrows, she hadn't realized they'd been snaking toward the back of the professor's house, but here was his fence!

"Maybe we can peek in!" Tessa said, trying to see between the slats. She moved along the fence. "I can't see anything. Can you?"

"Nope." The wood slat fence stood a good two feet higher than even Gus.

"Maybe there's a knot somewhere," Tessa hoped, scanning the planks from top to bottom. "Do you think—" she lowered her voice. "Do you think he has some kind of security system, like a hidden camera or something and can see us snooping around?"

Tessa looked up at the maple tree that towered above them and for a moment thought she saw a camera pointing down. But the thick leaves were blowing around too much to see clearly. She'd probably imagined it, but still she shivered at the possibility. "There's gotta be a way," Tessa said shaking off her worry. She crouched down, her cheek nearly on the pavement, and tried to see under the fence. "Urgh! Just grass!"

Suddenly, a section of the fence a few feet in front of her swung open.

Tessa sprang to her feet and started to walk toward the opening when a voice stopped her in her tracks.

"Well then," said a man they couldn't see. "Come in, come in."

CHAPTER 4

Tessa and Gus stared at the door that didn't hang by hinges but seemed suspended, floating open beside the fence.

"Don't stand there all day. Come in, I say!"

Gus and Tessa looked at each other. They couldn't see the professor, but Tessa thought his voice sounded friendly. She started toward the door.

"Are you sure?" Gus whispered. "What if this is a punishment for spying?" Tessa saw him rub his palms on his shorts, the way he did whenever he was nervous and his hands got sweaty.

"It isn't! This is our chance," Tessa whispered back craning her neck for a better view of the contraptions she could now see parts of through the opening. "We *have* to go in!"

"Ok fine. But text my mom so if we're abducted, she at least knows where we were last seen."

Tessa knew Gus was half-kidding, and also right. Tessa, being the only one of them with a phone, was in charge of parent-texting, so she quickly sent Mika their location, then pulled Gus through the gate with her.

As soon as they stepped into the yard, the door behind them vanished, and the fence became seamless once more. "We're trapped in here!" Gus hissed.

Tessa looked back at the smooth wall of boards. "That is so cool."

"It's NOT cool," Gus whispered harshly. But Tessa's attention had turned to the yard full of tinkering machines. They looked like wildly complicated marble shoots made of kids' building sets and metal piping, doweling rods and gyroscopes, and countless yards of metal track. The one in front of them stood about 20 feet high, and Tessa couldn't imagine how they hadn't seen it from the alley. Her eyes followed the narrow metal track as it rose steeply and plunged downward like a rollercoaster bending and winding away from them. Tunnels and swinging obstacles each moved to their own rhythms. Gus and Tessa stood transfixed. If they were in trouble, ncither of them could tear their eyes away from the fanciful bright machines to recognize it.

"What *are* these?" Tessa asked, finding her voice.

"Ahhhh, my inventions. These are my sight machines."

Tessa jumped to find Professor Henchworth standing beside her. She hadn't realized he'd come over. Up close, Tessa saw that he was a short man. His white wispy hair was a bit shaggy and curled at his ears, and his wide smile showed slightly crooked teeth. Though Tessa had always thought of him as rather an odd duck, she was surprised to see that his face was handsome with a close white beard and bright blue eyes. Though he was older, he seemed youthful and strong now that she looked directly at him. Just as Gus had remembered, the professor wore his brown tweed coat with two new pencils, eraser-side up, poking out of the breast pocket.

"I've been wondering when you'd come," he said.

"You have?" asked Tessa, surprised.

"Of course. I've known for a long time that it would be the two of you."

"That what would be the two of us?" But before the professor answered, a sound interrupted them.

Gus had picked up a small red rubber ball — Tessa

saw now that balls lay beside each invention — and plunked it into the wire basket of a machine on his left. The basket had swung toward a wooden maze-box that jiggled the ball through to a long slide. The slide ended in tight spirals, whirling the ball around so fast it blurred, and then spit it down a pipe where it rang a bell, and was finally sucked into a tube with a loud vacuuming noise. A second later they heard a "pop," and an eyepiece, like a pair of copper binoculars, sprang up at the far end of the invention.

Neither Tessa nor Gus moved.

"Go take a look," the professor said behind them.

Tessa and Gus exchanged glances and then slowly walked over to the eyepiece. "You go first, since you made it happen," Tessa said, elbowing Gus. Gus glared at her, then leaned over and peered into the binoculars attached to a post.

"Hey!" he cried after a second. "It's the towpath along the canal! That's where my dad takes Hodges and me to skip stones!"

"Ooooh! Let me see!" Tessa loved the towpath, too, and joined Gus and his little brother Hodges there sometimes. She leaned in for a peek, and then drew back. "This isn't the towpath! It's Buttercup Hill where we used to have that fort!" She checked again to make sure.

"No, I'm *sure* it's the towpath – "

"I'll have a turn." The professor walked over to where they stood. "Ahh," he said, peering in. "The brown wingback chair in the back of Holson's Books, just beside the biographies."

Tessa stared at him. "Is that what you see in there, Professor?"

"Every time!" he said.

"How can we see different things through the same lenses?" Gus asked.

The professor laughed gently. "So many questions. Of course."

Tessa looked again, and there was Buttercup Hill in bloom, the roots of the fallen tree where they'd once had a hideout, and where she often still went to be alone, in full view.

"Is the bookstore your favorite place, Professor?" Tessa asked, looking at him searchingly.

He nodded, his eyes twinkling.

"And this is mine. But how could *that*," she gestured toward the invention, "know what we like?"

"All good questions. It has to do with my study of sight," said the professor, as if this were a perfectly reasonable explanation. "There's always more than meets the eye."

Tessa could almost see the wheels turning in Gus's head, trying to make sense of the professor's words. "Do all of these inventions have eyepieces?" Gus asked, looking around.

"Yes, go see for yourselves."

Tessa and Gus began to walk around the yard, dropping balls into the contraptions and watching them whirl along wild tracks until copper eyepieces popped up. They couldn't imagine what more they'd see.

CHAPTER 5

Tessa and Gus explored the different inventions for what felt like hours. Through one invention, made out of bright plastic springs that stretched and twisted into tunnels, they saw blooper reels one after another: giggling babies burping, a chef tripping down the stairs with banana cream pies, a boat getting wedged on a sandbar and boomeranging a water skier around it. They laughed until their stomachs hurt.

The last invention was low and winding, made of dark wood with stretches of long metal piping. Tessa picked up the ball, a heavy silver marble, and released it along the tracks, listening to its slow roll until an eyepiece popped up. By the goose bumps that crawled along her arms and up her neck as she walked over, Tessa knew these machines did not work according to the science she learned in school.

As soon as she leaned down to look, Tessa could hear the scene she saw in the eyepiece perfectly. She wasn't wearing headphones but somehow knew the sound was only for her:

"It's fine!" Tessa was saying to Gus as she piled wadded paper and logs in the fireplace in her living room. "I do this all the time!" She felt a pang of guilt – she'd actually lit fires in the fireplace alone only once before. But she was sure her dad wouldn't care, and she knew how to do it. She struck one of the sparkler-length matches and watched the paper under the logs flare orange. "Hey Gus!" she said, swinging around, "I just remembered–"

"Tessa!" Gus shouted.

She turned back in time to see the long window curtain beside the fireplace roar with flames! Her match had caught it when she'd turned around.

Tessa jumped back as the flames surged. "I've got it!" Tessa dug frantically in her pocket, but her phone wasn't there. Flames licked the ceiling and started to char the rug. Gus stood frozen.

"Call 911!" Tessa yelled, even though she knew he didn't have a phone either. She ran into the kitchen, but the landline wasn't in its cradle.

Opening the cabinet doors, she pulled out the biggest pitcher she could find, and cranked on the faucet. As she plunged it into the water, the china pitcher hit the inside of the sink and cracked in pieces.

Smoke billowed into the kitchen. Gus ran through, covering his mouth with his shirt. "The ceiling's burning!" he screamed opening the backdoor. "We've gotta get out. We need your mom!" he yelled over his shoulder.

Tessa froze.

"Get your mom!!" Gus yelled again as he ran outside.

"I — I can't." The words felt like glue in her mouth and tears burned her eyes. Suddenly Tessa's phone rang from the windowsill. She hadn't seen it.

"Dad!" she screamed, grabbing it.

"Sorry but I'm leaving for Chicago — last minute —" the line cut out.

"Help!" Tessa screamed to the empty room. "Help!" she screamed, still holding her phone to her ear. The air burned with smoke, and fire leaped in through the kitchen door.

Tessa jerked her head back from the lenses, quickly smearing the tears that sprang from her eyes.

"Oh." The professor spoke close behind her. "That machine is a powerful one."

Tessa didn't say anything. Gus had told her to get her *mom* for help. Tessa's heart still throbbed. Of course Gus knew Tessa's mom was gone. He never would have said that. But, Tessa *had* needed her mom. And her dad. No one was there. She took a few deep breaths.

"This one shows us our fear," the professor said. His eyes were gentle as they looked at her.

Tessa didn't need him to explain. She knew it was true and that what the invention showed wasn't about fire. It was the fear of being left alone that still prickled her skin. What if something *did* happen one day and no one could help?

Gus's expression shook Tessa from her thoughts. He was frowning and looked worriedly at her. She forced a small smile.

"I'm not sure I want to look in that one," Gus said, glancing at the professor.

"Oh, go on," he urged. "It never hurts to recognize what we fear." The professor paused and looked at Tessa. "At least it never hurts more than the fear itself, which is already within you."

Gus held back for a moment, and then looked. After a few seconds he shoved the machine away and shook his head as if trying to shake out the scene. He didn't say anything.

Tessa wondered what he'd seen. Ever since his

grandparents had been in a car accident last year, Gus had been terrified that something would happen to his parents or his little brother. His grandparents had miraculously survived with only a couple of broken bones, but their car was unrecognizable, and the whole thing shook Gus up pretty badly. He didn't talk about it much, but every once in a while, he'd mention nightmares about accidents, and he always looked spooked. Tessa knew he feared something worse happening to someone he loved.

Gus's arms were crossed tightly across his chest and he stared at the grass at his feet. Tessa decided not to ask.

"It's a hard one," the professor said, gesturing toward the machine again. "It's never easy to look straight at what we fear. But," the professor paused, and Tessa reluctantly looked up at him. Out of the corner of her eye, she saw Gus do the same. "But, there is always an invitation when we face our fear: an invitation toward courage, or change, or some other surprise."

Tessa was about to ask how fear could be an invitation when her stomach grumbled loudly.

"On that note," the professor said in a cheery tone, nodding at Tessa, "why don't you join me for tea?"

CHAPTER 6

"Tea?" Gus asked, startled. His stomach obviously wasn't talking to him like Tessa's was.

Before he could say anything else, Tessa spoke up. "We'd love to!" He shot her a hard look.

"This may be our only chance," Tessa whispered, following the professor toward the wooden steps that led to his blue painted backdoor.

"Of course, check with your parents," said the professor knowingly, deadheading geraniums as he passed them.

"Oh, all right," Gus agreed, looking uneasy. "I'll text this time." Tessa passed him her phone.

Hi mom, tea at the professor's, k?

"Play-by-play of her son's massacre," he whispered to Tessa, as he stared at the phone for a reply.

Tessa heard the professor chuckle, though he surely was too far away to have heard Gus.

Tessa's phone dinged. "My mom's good with it," Gus said sounding almost disappointed. "And," his voice curved into a question as he read: "she said to tell you hello? Do you know my mom, Professor?"

"Oh my yes," he responded, smiling broadly and walking inside.

Gus's eyebrows shot up.

"No way!" Tessa laughed, following the professor through the door into a cozy eating area of low chairs with plush floral pillows, and a table set for three. In the center of the table sat a full pot of steaming tea and a plate with three little cakes.

Gus leaned closer to Tessa. "Did he know we were coming? How come there are *three* cakes? And how's the tea so hot?"

Just as they were about to sit down, Tessa and Gus simultaneously spotted a fat piece of blue chalk sitting on the counter and a blue arrow drawn on the floor that pointed to the table.

"You!?" Tessa said, her mouth hanging open.

The professor twinkled a smile and ducked into an adjoining room. "Please make yourselves comfortable and help yourselves," he called to them.

The chalk still didn't explain how the tea was so hot or who had put it on the table, but knowing the arrows came from the professor made Tessa restless with anticipation.

"But the arrows didn't even point to his house — they stopped at the corner," Gus whispered. Just then an orange cat jumped up next to him and stretched. Neither Tessa nor Gus had seen the cat come into the yard with them, or into the house, but it was definitely the same cat from the alley.

"Hi again," Gus said, scratching the cat under its chin. "You helped, too, huh?"

"This is *your* cat?" Tessa called incredulously.

"Oh! So you've met Meshugena!" the professor called from the other room where they heard him puttering around.

"Did he *send* this cat? And how could the professor have known we'd be in the alley?" Tessa whispered.

"A puzzle is only worth solving if you have to work for it," the professor's voice responded.

Tessa shot Gus a look. *How can he hear us?!* she mouthed, silently. There was no way the professor could hear them whispering from the other room, could he? Her eyes widened with excitement.

The kids leaned back on the squishy pillows waiting

for the professor to return and helped themselves to tea with milk and sugar cubes. They'd never tasted lemon cake like this that melted from tart to sweet as it hit their tongues.

Soon the professor appeared and popped a whole piece of cake in his mouth, his eyes laughing as he chewed the enormous bite.

"Professor," said Gus, "how'd you know we'd find your arrows?"

The professor smiled at the cat and swallowed the last of his confection. "First," he said, "I have something!" He pulled a small trinket from behind his back. It appeared to be a golden telescope but only a few inches long, exactly the length of the professor's palm. It was as wide around as a regular telescope, and Tessa could tell that, although it was so short, it was still collapsible.

"This is a vider," the professor said. "As you use it, you will begin to find answers to your questions."

"A vider?" Tess asked. "Sounds like a spider and a viper mixed – blech!" She made a face.

The professor chuckled. "It does, but you'll find there's no relation. The name stems from the Latin *Videre: to see*, and French *Vider: to empty*. For true sight, we must see well *and* empty ourselves of what we think we know. This will make more sense once you've used the vider."

"Used it how?" Tessa asked.

"To see, of course. Remember," continued the professor, "you will need to see quite a bit more if you're going to help us. Guard this vider, and use it well. Come along." He handed the vider to Gus and bustled out of the room.

"If we're going to help *who?*" asked Tessa, hurrying after him. But the professor had already opened the front door and was ushering them out. Before they knew it, the door clicked shut, and Tessa and Gus were standing on the front stoop, blinking in the brightness of the day.

CHAPTER 7

"Help who?" Tessa asked again. "What was he talking about!" Tessa stood facing the now-closed door.

Gus shook his head. "I dunno. He's so good at *not* answering questions." Gus looked through the vider. "I am glad he wasn't a murderer."

"I can't believe we were in his house!" Tessa exclaimed. "What *is* that thing?" she asked distractedly. "And what about his crazy inventions?"

"Do you think his cat is a robot?"

"I didn't. Until you said that." Tessa laughed. "What did he mean about seeing a lot more?"

Gus moved the vider up and down looking around with it. "This doesn't do anything." He handed it to Tessa.

"Is it a tiny telescope? A magnifier?" She pointed it at the street, the passing cars, and her shoes. "Huh... Nothing changes. Why'd he give this to us?" She turned it over in her hand. Her heart was just starting to calm from the adrenaline rush of the last hour. "It can't be for *nothing*," she insisted.

"No, not after all that stuff in his yard," Gus agreed.

"But," Tessa paused for a second. "Those inventions were cool, but they must be some kind of magic trick, right? Same with this?" She held up the vider.

"I dunno." Gus shrugged. "They seemed pretty real."

But as they walked, the vider, whatever it was, felt more like a cheap toy in Tessa's hand.

"Rink!" Tessa called, spotting a blond girl headed toward them carrying a jar of peanut butter with two spoons jutting out of it. Tessa handed the vider to Gus, who zipped it into his backpack, and waved.

"Want a snack?" Rink called out. "I was just on my way to your house, Tessa."

Rink and Tessa had been friends since fifth grade when Rink Trolly's family moved from Russia to a house down the street. Her real name was Radinka — everyone in her family had a Russian name — but her little sister called her Rink, so everyone else did too. She usually came over for a snack and to debrief the day, after she'd let her dog out.

Tessa loved Rink. With her broad-cheeked smile and wavy thick blonde hair, she seemed to have a solution for everything, from word problems to how the class could dominate the can drive. She spent a lot of time writing down "Life's Mysteries," as she called them, on her green-paged notepad: Why did Priscilla Simmons only wear bows on the right side of her head? Why did Edward Logger always smell a little bad? Why did Mrs. Finner always wear navy tights and black shoes — was she colorblind? Rink would *freak out* if Tessa told her what had just happened in the professor's yard. But for some reason, the experience felt too fresh to talk about. And too weird, so Tessa decided not to say anything. Not yet.

Tessa felt full from the lemon cake, but Gus reached past her and took a spoon out of the jar. "Thanks, Rink!" he said, putting the peanut butter in his mouth. "Crushees ma favit."

Rink laughed. "Mine too."

When they arrived at the alley between Tessa and Gus's houses, Samson, Gus's best friend from school, was already playing basketball.

"We're back, Mom!" Gus yelled generally toward his house as he instinctively held up his arms to block Samson. Samson passed the ball to Tessa who, though it would be a wild three-pointer, hurled the ball toward the hoop. It swished through the net. Samson whooped and rebounded the ball.

"Nice," he said, slapping Tessa's hand. Though Tessa was one of the shortest kids in the grade, she was a good shot and had been on the team for years.

"It's all you guys, today," Tessa called, feeling her curls bounce in every direction as she walked over to Rink. Normally she would have played longer, but today she needed her daily download with Rink about Samantha.

Tessa dropped her backpack and sat down against the brick wall next to Rink.

"Only four-and-a-half more hours of Samantha," Tessa said.

"One minute is too much Samantha," Rink responded.

As the youngest of three girls, Tessa knew how to stand up for herself, but standing up to Samantha was different. Samantha's dad was the guidance counselor at school, and all of the teachers seemed to think she was some kind of angel. She looked much older than she was, wore tons of eye makeup, and always had her bag loaded with gum that she gave out to her friends, even though gum-chewing wasn't allowed at MacArthur Elementary. Girls flocked to her, but Tessa was sure it was partly because they were scared of her. Samantha had always picked on someone, and no one wanted to be it.

"What were the CODs?" Rink asked. They'd started a daily ritual of recounting, as Rink fondly named them, Samantha's CODs — Crimes of the Day.

"She's become more subtle," Tessa explained, "which is actually worse. She used to tease me about Gus, you know, which was just stupid. But today she sat behind me in math, and every time Mr. Harvey turned around to write on the board, she'd lean forward and say something snarky." Tessa wrinkled her nose and in her best Samantha voice said, "'Nice miss at second base yesterday.' Did she not watch the rest of the game?? I brought in three runs!"

"Yeah, you actually had a great game," Rink agreed.

"And then she and her friends did their usual thing when I walked into History — and English and Science! Why do I have every class with her? They started whispering right away and looking me up and down."

"They're so immature," Rink said, in her most adult voice. It reminded Tessa of Rink's mom, and Tessa couldn't help but smile. "Can't they find something better to do? She's freakish!" Rink always ended their conversations about Samantha like that, and it was kind of perfect because, really, there wasn't much more to say. Rink gave Tessa a bear hug and picked up her half-empty jar of peanut butter. "I gotta get home," she said, "but I'll see you for the last day!! Dasvedanya!" she called in Russian.

"Dasvedanya!"

"Hey Gus," Tessa called as he missed a layup. "Got any new sketches?"

"Yeah," he panted. "My sketchbook's in my bag if you wanna look."

Tessa fished through Gus's backpack of crumpled papers, loose markers, and packages of cookies, and pulled out his sketchbook. Even in class, Gus always had a sketchbook opened beside whatever work he was doing. He especially loved drawing cartoons.

His latest drawings were in pencil. Tessa looked at one which must have been from the bus this morning: a cartoon of Samantha, her eyebrows raised, huge mouth screaming, pointy black boots kicked up, running, as she looked back over her shoulder at a towering vampire with fangs past its chin. Tessa smiled. The last drawing in the book said *ONE MORE DAY* in blocky letters around the edges of the paper, framing a cartoon of a mob of kids running out of the school building, arms in the air, with Gus, Samson, Rink, and Tessa in the front. It looked just like them. Tessa smiled at her own black hair, and the dark freckles he'd drawn across her face. In the picture, Samantha had been knocked down and sat at the edge of the paper with little birds flying around her head.

Tessa stood up and dropped Gus's sketchbook back in his bag. "See you guys tomorrow!" she called and headed toward the front of her house. Looking around, Tessa thought for the millionth time how she loved this neighborhood. The brick townhouses lined the streets, but it didn't look too clean and tidy. The brick was old and worn and made the houses look full of stories. Some had sprouting bushes or shaggy trees out front, and every spring the entire neighborhood erupted in so many azaleas that Tessa could forget she was in the city. But the maze of alleys reminded her, and they were her favorite part.

CHAPTER 8

Big old fashioned clocks still hung on the wall in each of Tessa's classrooms, and Tessa watched the red secondhand sweep slow circles. Only one minute and twenty, nineteen, eighteen seconds until the 12:35 bell and the end of school.

Concentrating on the second hand helped her tune out the whispers behind her. Tessa didn't even want to know what the girls were saying. Forty-five seconds, thirty-five, thirty. She watched the hand all the way to the twelve, then bolted from her chair as the bell rang.

"And that's the end of sixth grade!" Mrs. Bellmont, Tessa's English teacher, announced to the class. "Eager, aren't we?" She smiled at Tessa, who was already to the door, her backpack slung over her shoulder. Tessa ran down the stairs, pushed the metal bar on the heavy door, and she was free!

The weather this last week of school had been muggy, but today clouds covered the sky and made the air cooler. Tessa took a deep breath. She'd made it! She and Rink had already cleaned out their lockers before the first bell so they could leave as quickly as possible, and now Tessa leaned against the chain link fence and watched the sea of kids pour out the front door. In a second she spotted Rink's bright blond hair in the crowd and waved.

Rink broke free and headed toward Tessa, doing an exaggerated victory dance.

"Nice moves Trolly," said Samantha, who seemed to have materialized out of nowhere. "Hope you get to ring the bell this summer." She flashed a fake smile. The girls with her snickered, and Tessa heard Jane say, "I get it – Rink Trolly — ring the *trolley* bell." Tessa rolled her eyes.

Without a second look at Tessa, Samantha strutted away, announcing loudly to her groupies, "My mom's picking us up in the convertible and taking us straight to the mall. She said she'll pay for us *all* to get something!" Samantha exaggeratedly stepped sideways and bumped into Jaden, the boy she'd had a crush on all year. "Oh sorry!" she giggled, tossing her hair.

Tessa turned away. "Good riddance!"

Rink laughed a bright laugh. "My mom's picking me up in five," she said. Tessa knew Rink and her mom had a tradition of having lunch together on the last day of school to celebrate and to plan for sleep-away camp. This year Rink was going away for four weeks!

"Where are you going to lunch?" asked Tessa, feeling a throb of jealousy and wondering if she and her mom would have been having lunch together, too, if she were still here. Tessa pushed the thought away.

"House of Kabobs. Their rice is the best, and it reminds my mom of shashlik," said Rink. "Always shashlik with her!" Rink said smiling.

"Yeah," said Tessa, remembering the Memorial Day when Rink's family moved their grill to the front yard and made shashlik, grilled Russian kabobs, for the whole street. "At least it tastes really good."

Gus walked over to them. "Summmmmer!" he sang, slapping Rink and Tessa high fives.

A car pulled up and gave three short honks. "That's me!" said Rink. "We'll definitely see each other before I leave!" She gave Tessa a tight quick hug.

"Definitely!" said Tessa hugging Rink back. She paused. "You guys saved me this year." She looked between Rink and Gus and sudden tears prickled her eyes. "OK!" She clapped to distract herself and bellowed in her best announcer's voice, "Let's go do SUMMER!"

Rink smiled as her mom pulled up. "Love you! Meet at the pool this weekend! Dasvedanya!"

"Dasvedanya!" Tessa called back.

"Where to?" asked Gus, looking around at the near-ghost town school. "This place emptied fast!"

"*I* couldn't get out fast enough! So glad our parents didn't make us ride the bus today. Want to get gum?"

Gus started walking before he even nodded.

✳ ✳ ✳

The store on the corner a few blocks from school had a jar of the most fantastically huge pieces of grape bubblegum, wrapped like taffy, in a jar on the counter. Tessa and Gus liked to compete and see who could blow a bubble big enough to cover their entire face. Last summer, Tessa had blown a bubble so big that it had stuck in her bangs. Pulling and combing had only made it worse. She'd even tried using peanut butter and Vaseline to get it out, which was disgusting and didn't help. She'd had to cut the gum out, which had left her bangs so short they jutted straight out from her forehead.

But that didn't stop her from trying to beat Gus again.

Tessa pushed open the old door, and the bell jingled overhead. As she walked to the counter, she dug for crumpled dollars in the bottom of her backpack. Gus yanked a handful of quarters and the vider from his own bag. "Hey, remember this thing?" he asked, holding it out.

"That does not feel like it was yesterday!" Tessa said, as Gus paid for eight pieces of gum with his coins. Tessa gave up looking for dollars, and they each popped two pieces in their mouths and wandered further into the store.

Gus sampled from the boxes of berries they passed. "Berries in grape gum can only make it better," he said blowing a bubble that was swirled with strawberry juice and seeds.

"Disgusting!" Tessa cried.

"Maybe the vider works differently inside?" Gus asked, holding it up to his eye and looking around the store. "What the —"

CHAPTER 9

Gus was staring intently at a woman choosing cucumbers. "It's doing something."

"What's it doing?" Tessa bounced impatiently next to him.

"I dunno," said Gus lowering the vider and trying again. "That woman's all colors. But they're moving. It's cool."

"Let me see!" Tessa pulled his arm.

Gus raised and lowered the vider a few more times, then handed it to her.

"Woah!!!!" Tessa said looking at the same woman. "What *is* that?" Tessa couldn't see the woman's insides, not her organs or bones, but something else. Her body and head were filled with a cloudy substance. It was almost all yellow, but a stormy shade of yellow, peaked with greens and browns. The woman's forehead was furrowed — somehow Tessa could see both the outside and inside of her at once — and the stuff inside her head reminded Tessa of a churning ocean.

The woman glanced up. "Do you need something?" she asked in an irritated tone.

"OH, uh, I —sorry," Tessa stammered, backing awkwardly away. "Sorry." She and Gus ducked down the first aisle.

"I guess we were kind of obvious," said Gus.

"Awk-ward!" Tessa sang.

From where they stood, they could see the front of the store and the tall high school boy who bagged groceries. People always got mad at him for fumbling produce and packing the soft bread and bananas under heavy cans. Tessa looked at him through the vider and watched him change: the boy's whole body vibrated, and Tessa could almost hear a buzzing noise. No wonder the kid's hands shook when he bagged groceries; his whole body was full of a metallic static that shook even his eyes.

"Oh," said Tessa, "that looks like it feels awful." She handed the vider to Gus, who cringed as he looked at the shaking boy.

"What do I look like?" Tessa asked, brightening.

Gus turned the vider toward her. "WHOA!"

"What is it?" Tessa asked, bouncing up and down.

"Fire! Not actual fire, but flames! They're pink and red and orange — and gold! leaping all over the place."

"Can you see my face also?" she asked, sticking out her tongue.

"Yeah — Tessa!" She was making her zombie face and started laughing. "When you laugh, everything gets brighter for a second. Make another face!"

Tessa squatted down with her arms tucked in her armpits and walked like a duck until she lost her balance and knocked three cereal boxes to the floor with her knee. "Did it work?"

"Yeah," said Gus, laughing at Tessa as she scrambled to get the boxes back on the shelf, knocking another two off as she did.

"Let me see *you*!" Tessa said, hopping up. She snatched the vider from Gus. "Wooooooaaah. This thing is so coooooool."

"What do I look like?" Gus asked waving his arms around.

"Like a windmill," said Tessa, batting his swinging arms. "No but really, you're *bright*. It's hard to explain.

Everything's moving! Blue, all sorts of blues. And greens. It's like when we went whitewater rafting on the school campout — it's water like that. It's like there's a current, even though it's inside your body. So. Cool."

As Tessa and Gus moved through the store, Tessa imagined them full of flames and rapids and felt kind of proud.

Ahead of them, a woman stood at the deli counter ordering pastrami. She wore red lipstick and her bleach-blonde hair pulled tightly into a high ponytail. Her face had a striking quality and also a fierceness to it.

"Let's check her out," Gus suggested. As Tessa viewed her through the vider, the woman instantly became a black wisp of smoke and vanished. Tessa lowered the vider to see if the woman had moved, but she still stood in exactly the same place. Again Tessa looked through the vider, and again the woman instantly turned to smoke. "Crazy," muttered Tessa under her breath. She turned to the butcher. Blue and green orbs of all sizes filled his body like live bubbles. Unlike the stormy woman, his colors rose and popped in a cheery way. Tessa glanced back once more at the blond woman and, again, she poofed into smoke.

"What in the world?" wondered Tessa aloud.

Just as Gus was about to ask what she'd seen, the blond woman snapped her head around and glared at them so severely that the two children jumped back, turned around, and ran straight outside.

Gasping for breath at the end of the block, Tessa and Gus looked at each other. "We just ran away from a woman ordering pastrami!" Tessa burst out.

"She was terrifying!" Gus said, laughing. They collapsed on a bench, and Tessa unwrapped another piece of gum as Gus pulled out his sketchbook.

Tessa watched him draw a picture of the woman holding a giant plate of deli meat with laser beams coming out of her eyeballs. "She did glare that intensely," Tessa confirmed and told Gus how the woman had disappeared through the vider. "And it wasn't just once! I tried three times!"

"That's so cool," said Gus as the bubble he was blowing popped and stuck to the tip of his nose.

"Or weird," Tessa responded, frowning. She couldn't shake the uneasy feeling she had.

Gus closed his sketchbook as a group of little kids walked by, all holding loops on a rope. "Quick, the vider!" Gus said taking it and looking at the kids. "They're like jumpy gumballs!"

Walking home, Tessa and Gus passed a Jack Russell terrier tethered to a leash in its yard. "Does this work with animals?" Gus asked, answering his own question. He passed the vider to Tessa and they took turns watching the dog become a burst of green sparkler, flickering and flashing as it bared its teeth. The harder the terrier pulled against its leash and jumped up and down, the wilder the sparkler-dog shone.

CHAPTER 10

"Hey Mom!" Gus said, pushing open the screen door of his house.

"Hi Mika!" Tessa echoed.

"Happy summer!" Mika said, hugging Gus and then Tessa. Tall like Gus, but with dark brown hair she wore piled on top of her head, Mika was almost always smudged with something — paint or flour, pastels, or dirt from the yard — she was constantly creating.

Mika's art studio sat off the back of the kitchen. Canvases leaned against the walls. Tessa craned her neck to see how the one on the easel had changed since the last time she'd been there. These days Mika made huge abstract landscapes. She layered wallpaper, torn photographs, and scraps of fabric with heavy glue

and paint until each became a world of its own —
some felt familiar and some almost galactic.

"Any plans to see the professor again?" Mika asked.
Tessa thought Mika looked strangely eager and
glanced at Gus to see if he noticed.

"Nope," said Gus distractedly, digging through his
backpack.

Mika nodded. "There's banana bread under the foil
on the counter. Help yourselves!" she called as she
walked into her studio.

"Was she just weird?" Tessa asked, frowning. Mika
was *never* weird.

"Maybe," said Gus, glancing up at the doorway
where his mother had stood. "I asked her last night
how she knew the professor, and she said they've
known each other for years! Isn't *that* weird? How'd I
not know that? I've never seen them together. All this
time, I thought he was a stranger!"

"She's known him for years? Like she used to know
him lots of years ago? What else did she say!" Tessa
pressed.

"That was it," said Gus, shrugging as he pulled his
sketchbook and colored pencils from his backpack.
On the way home, he and Tessa had decided to keep a
record of everything they saw through the vider. Gus

added the stormy yellow woman from the grocery store and the happy bubbling butcher on the pages following the pastrami woman. He outlined the shaking bagger in jagged lines and scribbled green sparks with bared teeth jumping and prancing from one corner of a page to the other.

"The dog!" Tessa laughed. "What about us?"

"Oh yeah!" Gus said. "I forgot!" He drew Tessa's silhouette full of fire-colored pastels that he blended with his finger. The flames made her more beautiful than she felt. Then he pushed the sketchbook toward her. "Your turn," he said.

"Okaaaaay," she said taking the pencil. Her drawing efforts did not usually go as she intended. She giggled as she drew a lumpy outline of Gus's body and tried filling the shape with the lines of currents she'd seen. "It looks a little like a blue zebra blob, but you get the idea."

"Totally," Gus said smiling.

Mika stuck her head through the doorway. "Hey Gus, would you pop out back and see what your little brother's up to? I haven't heard anything from him for a little while."

Tessa thought "hearing from him" was a funny phrase to use for Gus's brother Hodges, since he was the quietest kid around, but Tessa knew Mika really meant for Gus to check on Lucy, the six-year-old neighbor Mika watched twice a week. She was outside with Hodges and could be up to just about anything.

"Sure," answered Gus, banging out the back door.

"So what's the last week been like?" Mika asked, leaning an elbow on the counter. Tessa was relieved to see that Mika's eyes were soft and she seemed unhurried. "How did the year end with Miss Samantha?"

"Not great," Tessa groaned. "But at least it ended!"

Mika put her arm around Tessa's shoulders and squeezed. She always seemed to respond just right. Though Tessa hadn't said it out loud yet, she'd started calling Mika "Tia Mika" in her head. The last few years Mika had really become like an aunt, but Tessa was still too nervous to voice it. She leaned into Mika's hug.

The screen door slammed behind Gus as he walked back in. "Hodges is her victim again," Gus reported.

"Oh dear," said Mika. "What's happening this time?"

Lucy loved performing and often spent her afternoons at the Tuckers' working on "shows." Whenever possible, she'd rope Hodges into helping.

"Well," said Gus, "I just heard Lucy tell Hodges to tap dance from one corner of the stage to the other, waving his hands in the air so they—" Gus paused to use air quotes around the word— *"shimmered,* singing *This Land is Your Land."* Gus shook his head as Mika and Tessa laughed.

"We have *got* to video that," Mika said, digging her phone out of her jeans pocket.

Imagining the scene was especially funny because five-year-old Hodges, with his short stout legs, ruddy cheeks, and perfectly round face, was the opposite of a performer. His dark brown, stick-straight hair fell almost to his eyes, and he hardly spoke at all. Whenever he got nervous, he pushed his hair off his forehead with the palm of his chubby hand. Gus grabbed Mika's phone, and he and Tessa sneaked out the front door, around the house, through the back gate, and up the ladder onto the platform Gus's dad had built in the pine tree. From there they could see the "stage," where Lucy was directing Hodges.

"Remember when we had our Sour Club up here?" Tessa asked. In fifth grade, she, Gus, Rink, and a couple other kids had started The Sour Club. Each week they'd brought whatever sour foods they could find and dared each other to eat spoonfuls.

"Remember the olive juice?"

"Ugh, yes! But that wasn't as bad as straight vinegar. It makes my eyes water just thinking about it —"

"Hodges!!" Tessa shrieked as a head popped through the trap door in the floor. "You gave me a heart attack!"

"Me too," said Gus, rubbing his head. "I jumped a foot."

"And hit your head against the tree trunk?" asked Tessa, suppressing a smile.

Gus nodded as Hodges smiled shyly.

"We didn't see you coming!" Tessa said. "You were just over there." She pointed to the grass where Lucy now stood alone, deep in a soliloquy. "Guess you got away." Tessa winked at him. The fact was, though Hodges was just a little kid, he could keep up with them and beat them at any target practice. He had near-perfect aim and always won at corn hole. Tessa liked his company.

"You're like a ninja with your silent approach." Gus said. "Guess you never know when that will come in handy."

CHAPTER 11

Tessa and Gus spent the rest of the afternoon hanging out in the tree waiting for dinner. Tonight was Wednesday, which meant Gus's dad was making macaroni and cheese, not the kind from the box, but the real, gooey, cheesy kind, with broccoli on the side, sprinkled with parmesan. It was Tessa's favorite meal. When Molly had left for school in the fall, Gus's parents, Mika and Marcus, had pretty much swept Tessa into their family. She ate dinner with them a lot on non-Loochie days when Cassie had practice and her dad worked late. Tonight Lucy's parents were working late, too, so she was staying for dinner, also.

At dinner, the Tuckers always said their Highs, Lows, and Buffalos of the day. Buffalos, something unexpected or funny, were Tessa's favorite part. As they shared around the table, Tessa knew she and Gus were thinking the same thing — this whole week had been a big fat buffalo, from the vider to the smoke woman. But could they say that out loud? *If there's any safe place, it's here,* Tessa thought, looking around the table. *But...*

"Who's first?" Gus's dad Marcus asked loudly. Marcus was big and broad with a shaved head — he called it shaved instead of bald — and a close cut beard. He had the broadest smile and loudest laugh of anyone Tessa knew. "Hodges," Marcus continued, "why don't you tell us your High?"

Hodges's face spread into a smile, and he held up a compass he was wearing on a string around his neck.

"Dad, isn't that the compass from the box on top of your dresser?" Gus asked. Marcus had a carved wooden box on his dresser that held his treasures. Even Tessa had looked through it before. She remembered a handful of foreign coins, a silver pen, two cigars wrapped in plastic that her dad had given Marcus the day Gus was born that they'd never smoked, and the old compass.

"Yep. Hodges was climbing up those drawers so often to see it, I thought one of these days he'd topple off and break his arm. So, I gave it to him."

Mika smiled at Hodges as he held the compass flat on his palm and watched the needle quiver and turn until it settled on North.

"Isn't it really old?" Gus asked.

"Ancient," said Marcus winking at Mika. "I've had it since before you were born."

Hodges beamed.

"What about your High, Gus?" Mika asked.

Gus talked about the dead roach he found in the bottom of his locker and how his math teacher had let them tear up their workbooks at the end of the period. Since he didn't bring up the vider, Tessa didn't either.

When they were done eating, Tessa and Gus threw the frisbee around in the street. It was late enough that there weren't many cars.

"When do you think we'll see Professor Hench-worth again?" Tessa asked, hurling the frisbee toward Gus. Just then her phone vibrated and she pulled it out. "My dad's home!" she exclaimed, reading his text. "Gotta go! You still have the vider, right?"

"Yeah," said Gus, pulling it out of his pocket.

"K. Keep it safe! I'll see you tomorrow!"

"It'll be summer!" Gus called after her.

✳ ✳ ✳

"Dad?" Tessa called as she pushed the front door open. She heard footsteps above her.

"How was the last day of school?" her dad Adam called as he jogged down the stairs and wrapped her in a hug. Tessa leaned into his chest and squeezed. "I lit the citronella candles on the porch, which should at least keep a few of the mosquitoes away, so we can sit out there and you can tell me about it," he said.

Tessa followed her dad into the kitchen where he'd already poured her a big icy glass of lemonade, which was unusual for after dinner. "I figured it could be our dessert," he explained as he pushed the screen door open with his shoulder. "Last day! So tell me." They settled onto the muggy, golden-lit porch.

Someone had once said her dad had "kind eyes," and looking at him, Tessa could see it. Maybe the soft wrinkles made it look like he was always smiling, or was it the shape of his eyes? Gus would know. She watched the wrinkles around his mouth deepen as he smiled, and her body relaxed. Looking at him, she wished they could stay out here on the porch for days, just the two of them, without his having to leave for work.

She took a long cold sip and started talking. "So school ended, and Samantha blah blah blah — same as always." Her Dad smiled knowingly. "But I did forget to tell that you that Gus and I met Professor Henchworth the other day! It was kind of our summer goal."

"Oh wow," said her dad. "I haven't heard that name for ages." He got a faraway look on his face.

"What do you mean?"

"Oh — a long time ago, we used to know him."

"You did?! Mika said that, too!" Tessa exclaimed.

"Yeah —" he got that look again. "A long time ago." Adam's phone rang, and Tessa braced herself as he pulled it out of his shirt pocket. Usually if someone called this late, he had to take the call and would talk for a while.

Adam glanced at the number, "Ugh! I have to grab this. So sorry, T!" He smiled apologetically and stood up, walking to the edge of the porch. "Hello..." he said into his phone.

Tessa watched how his white shirt glowed in the evening light. She waited a few minutes to see if he'd hang up, but he didn't. Then she walked to the door. Her dad blew her a kiss, pointed to the phone and shrugged apologetically as if to say "this guy just keeps talking." Tessa gave a small wave and left to go read in her bed alone.

CHAPTER 12

"What kind of camp starts in the middle of the week *and* the day after school gets out?" Tessa asked Gus as they walked to Jetties Sandwich Shop. "That's so messed up!"

"Yeah, I know Samson's a baseball fanatic and everything, but come on! You don't need to start camp the day after school's out! Is Rink coming?"

"No, she can't either. She's running errands with her mom. She leaves for sleepaway camp on Monday."

"Too bad. We can take pictures of our sandwich and email it to her at camp — it'll make her want to come home."

"Or we could mail her the empty bag of our salt and vinegar chips," Tessa said. "It would be a great envelope. But kind of greasy. And it would definitely smell!" Even though Tessa mostly emailed Rink at camp, she still liked finding creative ways to mail letters and packages. She was the most faithful camp-letter-writer she knew.

As far as Tessa was concerned, Jetties was one of the best parts of summer. Neither Tessa nor Gus ate there much during the school year because it was a little too far to walk to after school, but during summer, they pooled their money at least once a week to pick up their favorite sandwich: roast beef and horseradish on pumpernickel with extra pickles, and always a bag of salt and vinegar chips. Both Samson and Rink had written off everything sour after The Sour Club, so they usually ordered turkey or grilled cheese. But Tessa and Gus both still loved their Sour Club throwback and had perfected their order.

The kids sat at the small table and chairs by the window. Tessa was just licking the last of the vinegar-y salt off her fingers when she felt someone staring at her. She looked up and saw the blond pastrami-woman from the market standing on the other side of the restaurant looking at her. When the woman glanced down at the order form she was filling out, Tessa kicked Gus under the table.

"OUCH!"

"Quiet!! It's her! The woman!" Tessa hissed.

"What woman?"

"The smoke woman!"

Gus turned slowly around pretending to look out the window.

"I want to see her through the vider," he whispered. But right then the woman glanced up again. "She's staring at us."

"I'm on it!" Tessa jumped up, walked a few steps, and then tripped terrifically, sprawling on the floor and knocking a chair over. It was the perfect diversion. Gus whipped the vider from his pocket and looked over at the woman who, like everyone else in the restaurant, was staring at Tessa with alarm. Instantly, Gus saw the woman turn to smoke.

"Whoa," he put the vider back in his pocket just as the woman caught his eye. Chills ran up his arms. "Aaaaaand it's time to go!" He jumped up, grabbed the rest of their sandwich, pulled Tessa off the floor, and the two of them pushed open the heavy door and left.

"Excellent fall, Tessa! That was one of your best!" Gus congratulated her.

"Thanks," Tessa grinned. Last summer she'd spent

a week at clowning and miming camp and learned all sorts of stunts and falls. She'd practiced faithfully, and Gus had watched numerous attempts. "Did you see her?"

"Yeah! It was just like you said — smoke! And then she looked right at me."

"Yeah, there's something sinister about her." Tessa had loved the word sinister from the day she'd learned it and worked it into conversations whenever she could.

As soon as they were safely around the corner, Gus and Tessa sat on a bench to finish their sandwich. Gus took the vider out and watched the string of people walking by on the other side of the street. "Woah! Check out *that* guy!" He passed the vider to Tessa, who aimed it at a stocky man walking fast with hard steps. Through the eyepiece his skin was seething, like molten rock, black but with cracks that kept opening and closing all over revealing fiery lava underneath. "I wouldn't want to be wherever he's going. He could blow any second."

"No kidding. What about that one?" A boy across the street, a bit older than they were, dragged his feet keeping his eyes on the ground. Tessa looked at him.

"That one's sad," she said. "He's almost invisible."

Through the vider she could see a thin white outline of the boy. The murky dark blue that filled him was nearly transparent. "Doesn't it kind of seem private, what we're seeing? I mean, maybe that boy wouldn't want us to see him like this?" Tessa said.

"Maybe he doesn't even know he looks like that," said Gus. They took turns with the vider watching the people who passed transform. All of a sudden, Tessa gasped. She had the vider up to her eye and was pointing it at Michael. Michael was a guy who almost always stood at the traffic light at the corner asking for money. Gus's dad, who worked with refugee families and seemed to know everyone around, had introduced them to him once. Michael had shuffled his feet and hadn't said much, but now Tessa stared.

"He's — I mean — well, you've gotta see!" she shoved the vider into Gus's hand.

Gus couldn't have prepared himself for the sight. There was Michael, but it wasn't Michael. The man glowed with a substance so blindingly bright that it was hard to make out the outline of his body. He wore bright fatigues and a helmet, boots laced up his shins, and rather than his usual slumped posture, the thick light through his body made him appear strong and tall.

Michael faced them, smiled, and walked away. Gus watched until he was out of sight.

$$* * *$$

Back at Gus's house they sat huddled over his sketchbook, deep in thought. Gus sketched the woman from the restaurant, again with laser-beam-eyes that made smoking holes in Tessa and Gus's sandwich. Next, he drew the string of people on the sidewalk, and finally, Michael. Gus tried several times, but couldn't quite figure out how to make the image bright enough. Finally, he filled the background with charcoal smudges and left the shape of Michael's body as white paper. He'd nearly completed it when Tessa's phone rang.

Tessa's screen filled with a picture of Rink's face. "I'm going to answer really quick."

Gus nodded and kept messing with his sketch.

The good thing about Rink is that she always got straight to the point and talked fast. "Hey Rink," Tessa said.

"Hey, so get this! I was at the mall with my mom today to get new shorts for camp — I've outgrown all of mine but two pairs — anyway, we stopped to get a pretzel in front of the tanning place and guess what?"

"They were out of mustard?" Tessa guessed.

"No! Samantha was *in* the tanning place getting fake-tanned! Gross, right? Who in their right mind pays to get skin cancer? And who our *age* goes tanning in the first place? It was so totally Samantha."

"She's the *worst*. At least that explains why she's so freakishly tan all the time. She said it's because she's Italian." Both girls laughed.

"She actually doesn't even look a tiny bit Italian," Rink confirmed. "Ok, I've got to go to dinner. Talk to you tomorrow! Dasvedanya!"

"Dasvedanya!"

"Samantha report?" Gus asked.

"Yeah, fake tanning at the mall." Tessa flopped back into Gus's chair and rolled her eyes. Then she surveyed Gus's finished picture. He'd captured everyone. "Now what? That weird lady, Michael in glowing combat boots, all those people — what are we supposed to do with these?"

As they looked over the page, neither of them had any idea.

CHAPTER 13

On Thursday night, Tessa figured she could save the dinner Loochie made for leftovers the next day, and she ate dinner again with Gus's family — grilled chicken legs, corn on the cob, and watermelon slices. Tessa knew Gus loved this meal because he could eat it all with his hands.

"Hodges, tell us one fun thing about camp today," Mika said, rolling her corn in the butter.

"What camp are you doing?" Tessa asked, trying half-successfully to stuff the big bite of chicken she'd taken into her cheek while she spoke.

"Explore DC," Hodges said.

"It's a summer kickoff, just for a few days this week. They take a different field trip each day," Mika said. "Yesterday they went to Roosevelt Island and today to the East Wing of the National Gallery." Her eyes smiled at Tessa.

"Oh! Did you see my dad?" Tessa asked eagerly. She knew he sometimes helped with the educational program at the museum as part of his job.

Hodges nodded proudly. "We made Matisse."

"That's my favorite! You're lucky you got to see that exhibit!" Tessa knew a lot about the museum from her dad. The rooms on the top floor that held Matisse's huge paper cut-outs only stayed open only for a few hours a day because of the light exposure, so lots of people never saw them. "Did you see the one that looks like a window full of sea creatures?"

Hodges looked at her and squinted like he was thinking hard.

"That's just how I think of it," she said smiling. "It's really called Christmas Night, but in French. I'll show you a picture later."

"And what's new with you two?" Mika asked.

"Well, we've been messing around with this thing the professor gave us," Gus said.

"Oh?" Mika leaned forward. "What thing?"

"He says he studies sight," said Gus, digging in his pocket. "We don't really know what that means, but he gave us this." Gus pulled out the vider.

Mika's eyebrows shot up, and she looked at Marcus with alarm for a moment, then turned back to Gus. "What — what do you — how — " she stuttered.

Tessa and Gus exchanged glances. Mika was never at a loss for words.

"What's it do?" asked Marcus, rescuing her.

"Well," Tessa said, looking to Gus for help. "It shows us what people are like, I guess?"

"It sounds kind of weird. But — here," Gus said, "I'll show you." He held the vider up and looked at his brother, then through a half-laugh said, "Hodges, you're so cute!" Hodges raised his eyebrows. "You look like a toasted marshmallow! That really good golden puffy kind. Check him out, Tessa."

Tessa laughed. "Exactly that!" Then she turned to Mika who still had a strained expression on her face. "Woah, Mika! You're like a forest or forest floor — all moss and vines," Tessa reached out and blindly felt for the tangle of growth and instead hit Mika's shoulder and almost swatted her in the face. "Sorry!" Tessa said, lowering the vider. "You were a jungle!" Mika still looked a bit stunned but her eyes had brightened, and she was smiling now. Tessa turned to Gus's dad. "Marcus," Tessa said, watching him grin. "You look… folded. Gus, how would you describe this?" she passed him the vider.

"You do — like vellum origami that lets the light through in all different shades. Cool, Dad."

Tessa nodded. *Vellum, that see-through paper. Yes, that's just what he looked like.*

"Want to try it?" Gus handed Marcus the vider.

"Oh, it's heavier—" he stopped abruptly and looked at Mika.

"Heavier?" Gus asked.

Marcus shook his head and smiled as he looked through. Then he laughed a great big guffawing laugh and leaned over to squeeze Hodges. "I can't help it!" Marcus said. "It's the marshmallow!" He laughed again.

"Hodges, you try it," Marcus suggested, tossing the vider to him.

Hodges looked, then smiled and shrugged.

"What do I look like, Hodges?" said Gus.

"Same," he said.

"Same? Look right through it," Gus instructed, even though Hodges already had his eye pushed against the eyepiece.

"Same. Like the creek."

"Same?" Tessa looked at Gus in confusion. He *had* looked like the creek, but Tessa had a feeling that if she asked, Hodges wouldn't explain what he meant.

Mika was still surprisingly quiet, and Tessa didn't know how to read it.

"May I?" Mika said finally, reaching out her hand to Hodges. She paused and seemed to weigh the vider in her hand. She caught Marcus's eye for a long moment and then took her turn. She instantly lit up. "Yes!" she said looking around the room. "Gus!" She stared at him, and her eyes brimmed with tears. "Oh Hodges! Marcus! Tessa! You're all so beautiful!"

"Mom!" said Gus, surprised. Tessa couldn't help laughing at Mika's excitement.

"Really! You've got to *look*," Mika said, "*really* look."

"We did look," Gus protested.

"But stay with it," Mika said. She stared at them each for a long moment, then handed the vider back to Tessa.

Tessa watched Mika turn shadowy and verdant again. "Keep looking," she heard Mika say. Tessa focused hard on the beautiful woodsy person in front of her. She saw Mika's eyes wide and happy. Tessa kept looking. It felt a little awkward to be staring, but the eagerness on Mika's face made it ok. The longer Tessa looked, the more beautiful and mossy Mika became, until Tessa thought she could smell the damp forest floor and hear leaves rustle. Suddenly a wave of feeling surged through her. Joy was the best word for it, but it was achy, too, the way she felt on the last day at the beach when her favorite week was about to end. Her chest felt full enough to burst, and when she lowered the vider she found she was out of breath. "Woah," Tessa said. "I had to stop!"

"Yes!" Mika nodded. "It's powerful to look so deeply at someone," she said. "Keep that thing safe."

"You have to try," Tessa urged Gus, almost breathless. "Your mom's right, look longer."

For the rest of dinner, they passed the vider around. "I can't look at you for longer than a few seconds," said Gus to his mom. "At any of you."

"I know what you mean," said Marcus. "It's like looking at each other naked."

"Dad! Gross!" Gus said.

Marcus laughed his big laugh again. "No, I mean that through the vider we see each other without all the distractions. We *really* see each other."

"And," Mika added, "when we look at people we love that closely, we feel such deep affection that it's hard to keep looking. Love that deep feels bittersweet."

Bittersweet, Tessa thought. *So good, but possible to lose.*

* ✳ *

Later that night, Tessa and Gus stood on the side-walk trying to catch fireflies in one hand without crushing them. "That was crazy," Gus said.

"Yeah, what *is* this thing," Tessa asked, trying to follow the fireflies with the lens as they moved and disappeared in the darkness. "It's more intense that I thought."

"Yeah, even my parents got into it." Gus paused for a second. "But they acted kinda weird, right?"

"Yeah, they kept looking at each other, but then not saying anything. They're never like that." Tessa was twirling the vider in her hand and stopped suddenly. "What if we *do* lose this?" she asked, thinking of all the times she'd misplaced her phone this week.

"We can't," Gus said definitively. "Should I hang on to it? We can't call it!"

"Ha ha." Tessa suddenly swiped her hand through the air and when she opened her fist, she held three fireflies, still alive. "A record!" she yelled.

CHAPTER 14

As Tessa arrived at Gus's house, she heard Lucy yell from the front porch where she was dancing around Hodges. "YES! Milk and honey! That was so fast!"

Tessa turned to see Gus walking up empty handed. "Oh!" he huffed. "I, uh, forgot the groceries!"

"You *forgot* them? How do you go to the grocery store and forget your groceries?" Lucy asked, giggling.

"What's going on?" Tessa asked, looking between them.

"It's a long story," said Gus, gesturing for Tessa to follow him. "Uh, Lucy, tell my mom we're going back to get the stuff. Be home in a sec. Sorry about that!"

"OK, Mr. Forgetful. Don't forget where your house is when you come home!"

"Funny!" Gus called as he and Tessa started back up the block.

"What's going on?" Tessa asked for the second time. Gus had a startled look in his eyes.

"My mom sent me to get stuff for tea, but when I was at the store, I saw her! She was in line right behind me!"

"Who was?" Tessa asked eagerly.

"The smoke woman!" Gus wheeled around at the sound of footsteps behind them, but it was only Hodges. "Oh," said Gus, heaving a sigh of relief. "I thought you were someone else."

Hodges looked up at his brother and kept walking.

"Ok, I guess you can come with us," Gus said.

"Go on!" Tessa was dying to hear more.

"Well, she was right next to me, and every time she talked, I felt freezing, like my veins were ice —"

"She *talked* to you!? What did she say?"

"She smiled a lot and acted like we were friends. She said her name's Allergia Knights— what kind of name is *Allergia*? It's like algae! Or allergies! Anyway, then she tried to shake my hand and…" He looked like he was deciding whether or not to finish the story. "And I dropped the stuff I was buying and ran out of the store. I know it sounds stupid! But you should have been there! This woman is creepy. And she has this super-intense stare."

"Yeah, I could tell that from a mile away. Too bad you didn't have the vider!"

"I know."

"Who's Allergia?" Tessa and Gus had promptly forgotten Hodges was with them so hadn't thought twice about talking freely in front of him.

"Ummm," said Tessa. She looked at Gus questioningly.

"Ok?" Gus said looking sideways at Hodges. "Ok. But Hodges, don't say we didn't warn you. This all sounds crazy because it *is* all crazy." As they walked to the store, Tessa and Gus told Hodges the whole story, from going to Professor Henchworth's house to the laser-beam-staring Allergia Knights turning into smoke. Hodges listened.

"What if she's still in the store?" Tessa said abruptly.

"I was thinking about that, too. I think if we see her, we'll know she's been waiting for us, and we run. We can go get honey at 7-11."

But when they reached the store, Allergia Knights was nowhere to be found, and the cashier holding Gus's bag was chuckling. "If I'd made that woman as mad as you did, I would've run, too! I don't know what you said to her, but she looked like she could spit nails when you left. She took off right behind you!"

Gus cringed. That woman probably *could* spit nails. "Thanks for keeping my bag for me."

"No problem. Have a good one, and stay outta trouble!"

Tessa wondered if they could.

✳ ✳ ✳

As they stepped outside, Tessa stopped in her tracks. Diagonally across the street from them stood Samantha Shaw and her mother. Samantha's parents were divorced, and she lived with her dad. Tessa had never seen her mom before, but she was as beautiful as people said. Standing there with their glossy hair down their backs in the shade of a gingko tree, the scene looked like it could have been torn from a magazine. Tessa couldn't hear anything from where she stood, but she noticed they were both frowning.

Out of curiosity, Tessa fished the vider from her pocket and looked through it just as Samantha started talking. Words left Samatha's mouth as flat white sheets of paper and floated to the ground. As her mother answered her, Samantha's spoken papers crumpled and flew from the ground back into Samantha's mouth, forcing their way down her throat.

It looked painful. Tessa noticed then that the thin outline of Samantha's body was crammed with crushed and crumpled papers. Each time Samantha spoke, another clean piece of paper sailed to the ground, and every time her mother responded, the paper crumpled again by itself and flew back inside Samantha's mouth.

Tessa peeled her eyes away from Samantha to look at Samantha's mother. Her body seemed to be made of steel from the top of her head to her feet, and though Tessa was sure there must be something inside her — she'd seen that so many times this week — she couldn't see anything through the metal. Tessa turned back to Samantha standing stiffly in front of her mother and could almost feel the constriction of all that paper packed inside her.

"I wasn't expecting that," Tessa said softly, handing the vider to Gus. She was surprised to feel a tight sadness in her own chest.

CHAPTER 15

No one said much on the walk home. Tessa kept thinking about Samantha looking so helpless and all that crumpled paper jammed in her body, and Gus kept looking over his shoulder to check if Allergia Knights was following them.

"I think we should go back to the professor's house," Gus asserted. "Maybe he'll tell us more about this thing. Are we supposed to do anything else with it?"

"Good idea," Tessa said. "We haven't even seen him once since he gave us the vider, not even in the alley. What's he been doing?"

"Could I try?" Hodges's voice, again, took them by surprise, and Tessa saw him looking at the vider in her hand.

"Uh, sure," Tessa said glancing at Gus who nodded his agreement.

Hodges took it carefully and looked at the few people walking up the other side of the street: a woman with a stroller, another woman carrying a briefcase, a man walking a dog. Tessa and Gus waited for Hodges's squeal of surprise, but Hodges stayed quiet.

"Is it doing anything this time?" Gus asked.

Hodges shook his head.

"Look at the *people*. The vider shows their feelings." Neither Gus nor Tessa had said that aloud yet, but as soon as Gus articulated it, they both knew that was exactly what the vider did. It was showing them how people felt on the inside.

"Hmm… same," Hodges said, shrugging.

"Really?" Gus raised his eyebrows. "Maybe it isn't working. Try looking at that baby."

Hodges face broke into a big smile. "Baby!"

"Does it look pink and fluffy?" Tessa asked.

"Yeah. Normal."

"Normal? Hodges—"

"Do you ever go there?" Hodges interrupted excitedly.

They looked across the street to where Hodges was pointing the vider. Cars were parked beside the city park. There was a cracked blacktop and a low brick community center. "Into the community center?" Gus asked doubtfully.

"No, that *doorway*." Hodges's voice had a breathless quality to it.

"What doorway? The gate to the blacktop?" Tessa asked doubtfully.

"No, the huge one," Hodges said pointing.

"Wait," said Tessa. "Put down the vider. Can you still see it?"

Hodges shook his head.

"Let me look." Tessa took the vider but could only see the other side of the street. "You try." She said handing it to Gus.

"I don't see anything either," he said. "Describe what you see, exactly, Hodges."

Hodges looked through the vider again. "Giant door. Blue light. Stars. Grass. Path."

Tessa and Gus weren't sure what to think. Hodges usually said so little, and now he was describing things that weren't there. Did he think they were making up stories? From his serious expression and the way his forehead creased as he described what he saw, it didn't seem like Hodges was joking.

"We can't see that, Hodges," Gus said.

Hodges looked surprised for a moment and then said, "Let's go." Before anyone could argue, Hodges crossed the street and disappeared.

CHAPTER 16

"Hodges!!" Gus yelled, his eyes frantically scanning the other side of the street.

"Hodges!" Tessa called.

"Hodddddges!!" Gus's voice sounded as scared as Tessa felt. Gus stood staring at the park. His voice came out as a whisper. "He's gone."

Tessa felt her chest tighten. "He can't be." But he wasn't in front of them anymore.

"Hodddddggggges!!" Gus screamed.

A woman pushing a stroller glared at them with alarm.

Suddenly Hodges's head appeared, just his head hanging in the air. "You sound worried," he said.

"Hodges?" The color drained from Gus's face. "Are you — where are you? Are you ok?" They rushed across the street toward his floating head.

"Wha— Where's your body!?" Tessa yelled.

"Here. Come on." And with that, Hodges's two hands appeared below his head and reached for Gus and Tessa.

The moment Hodges touched them, Tessa and Gus could see. Hodges stood in an enormous wooden doorframe, and through it lay an entirely different world. As Hodges had described, the sky was deep blue like night, but somehow brilliantly bright, flooded with bold stars. The grass was vibrant, too, bright green as if it were full of sunlight, and behind it grew a dense wood. There was the path Hodges had mentioned, smooth and inviting. It cut through the grasses and disappeared over a hill.

"Come on!" Hodges said, again, and without really thinking, the other two stepped through the doorframe and followed him.

Once inside, Tessa found the world even richer than she'd thought. The colors were intoxicating and the smell of the grass so clean and summer-sweet she wanted to lie down in it. A slight breeze stirred the air and made the stars twinkle. How could it be night and so bright at once? They followed the path as it curved up and over a hill. Tessa felt as though she could walk for miles here on the springy ground. To their right, long grass blew lazily in a rolling flowered field, and Tessa could smell the damp earth and the shaggy trees in the woods beyond.

Gus kicked a rock along the path, and every time it bounced, it seemed to strike a low note, like it was bouncing on a wooden xylophone.

As they walked, Hodges made little noises that sounded like squeals of laughter.

"What are you doing?" Gus finally asked, turning to see Hodges wave at the empty field.

"Saying hi," said Hodges.

"To the grass?"

"No! Spegatrontus. Packasindrias!" He pointed.

"What?" Gus asked skeptically.

"The books!"

Gus stared blankly at his brother.

"*Mom's*," Hodges urged.

Gus and Tessa looked out at the field, spectacular but empty.

"Are you talking about flowers?" Tessa asked.

Hodges shook his head. "You *know*," he persisted, looking at his brother. "Mom's *books*."

A note of understanding crossed Gus's face. "The creatures Mom made up?"

"She didn't," said Hodges pointing now to the air. "Treetos!"

Gus opened his mouth and then closed it.

Tessa leaned over. "Do you know what he's talking about?"

"Sort of. There are these picture books my mom made when I was little about all these white creatures with funny names. I think Hodges still reads them. I guess he's pretending they're here?" Gus frowned as he watched Hodges wave toward the trees again.

Just then they rounded a bend, and there in the middle of the path sat a small table where Professor Argus Henchworth was seated!

"Children!" he called.

"Professor Henchworth!" Tessa broke into a run. "I'm so glad to see you! We were just heading to your house when we found this huge door!"

"Well I've been waiting for you! There's so much to talk about!" They spotted four steaming cups of tea, a bowl of brown crystalized sugar cubes, and a pitcher of milk. Again Tessa wondered how he'd known they were coming! Four plates were set with towers of chicken salad sandwiches, poppy seed cakes, and deep red cherries.

The children hadn't realized how hungry they'd

grown, but seeing the food reminded them they'd never had tea earlier, and, in fact, Gus was still carrying the grocery bag of honey and milk! They settled around the table and gratefully helped themselves.

"Hodges, I presume," said the professor looking into the boy's round face.

Hodges smiled through a mouthful of cake.

"Good finally to lay my eyes upon you, lad," said the professor with a smile. The two studied each other closely, almost as if communicating, before the professor turned back to Tessa and Gus. "And you both! I can see you've been using the vider as well."

"You can *see* we've been using it?" Tessa asked.

Gus cut in, "I think we're beginning to understand it. It shows how people feel."

"Yeah," Tessa agreed, nodding. "It's like we can see what they're like inside."

"Yes," said the professor with a small smile. "Yes."

CHAPTER 17

"We haven't seen you for days, Professor! Where've you been?" Gus asked.

"We have a zillion questions!" Tessa chimed in.

"Oh yes?" said the professor, smiling at their eagerness. "I haven't had much time for my inventions these days. Much is unbalanced. The danger is increasing." He looked intently at them.

"Danger?" Tessa said, pausing to take in her surroundings. As they'd been sitting, the sky, in a short time, had sweetened to pinks and golds and then to a high midday blue that nearly sang with clarity. Though they couldn't see a sun in the sky, warm light lit everything. Yellow flowers no bigger than fingertips, millions of them, had opened across the grass among floppy orange blossoms that seemed to hold light themselves. Nothing here *looked* dangerous.

"You haven't seen me," the professor continued, "because you haven't yet seen here."

"Where *is* here, Professor?" asked Tessa as she watched the trees right above them open wide fragrant white flowers as if in fast-forward. They laced the air with a sweet scent like jasmine.

"Here?" the professor asked. "Why 'here' is just where you began. You are in the same place, but now you're seeing the unseen layer. This is the world you always live in, but usually you see only the surface. Right now, we are in my back yard!" He looked delighted, and Hodges nodded. Instantly the children could see a shimmering outline of the professor's house, but as quickly as it came, the vision faded.

"Full existence means inhabiting both the Seen and Unseen simultaneously," the professor continued. "The barrier between the two is very thin, you know. Humans have a habit of relying solely on the eyes, but more, of course, exists to be discovered."

"Is that why you gave us the vider?" Gus asked. "So we could come here—" He corrected himself, "or *see* here?"

"Yes," said the professor. "Partly. I'll explain as quickly as I can. Our time together may be quite brief.

There is much instability these days between the Seen and the Unseen.

"When you were at my house that afternoon, Tessa and Gus, you looked into the inventions and could see something different than what was right before you, correct?"

They nodded.

"Those inventions were a tiny taste of sight's complexity. As you looked at your own fear, for example, you saw more deeply into yourselves, just as the vider has let you see more deeply into other people.

"But there's an invention far more powerful than any of mine! It's called The Great Invention, and every human sees through it."

"Wait. You're saying that *every* human sees through an *invention*?" asked Tessa, confused. "But that's impossible!" Tessa didn't mean to be argumentative but could feel her impatience trigger. She hated when she didn't understand something.

"Stay with me, Tessa," the professor urged. "This isn't an invention you put your eye up to, like a vider. The Great Invention balances the barrier between the Seen and Unseen. It allows people to see with their eyes, of course, but it also enables them to see with their hearts."

Gus and Tessa surveyed the sweeping fields of sweet grass and for a brief second, Tessa could see green currents inside Gus and a flicker of Hodge's soft white. "OK," said Tessa slowly. "So, seeing with the vider is seeing with the heart? It's seeing *inside*. That kind of makes sense."

"If there were no Great Invention," the professor continued, "humans would live only with eyesight. Think of that! They'd make all their judgments about the *outsides* of people. They would never have compassion! No one would truly know another person. In short, real love couldn't exist.

"On the other hand, if the barrier were too thin, humans would see as you've been seeing through the vider, and even more intimately than that. Seeing into others so easily would be dangerous; we'd forget what a rare gift it is to know another person's heart and mind. That is why we need The Great Invention because it balances us. It allows us to know each other deeply *and* to work hard to do so.

"Now, a few people have been given the gift of seeing fully without a vider. We call them Wholehearteds — Hodges knows this."

"Hodges?" Tessa asked, startled. She looked at

Hodges as if she were seeing him for the first time. The professor smiled again, and Tessa saw Gus's mouth fall open in surprise.

"The Wholehearteds," continued the professor, "become the teachers of the world. They help people enjoy this beautiful age we live in called The Age of Heart-Sight, where we have both the Seen and Unseen worlds at once, balanced. But if that balance were to change…" his voice trailed off.

"*Could* it change?" Tessa asked at the same time that Gus exclaimed, "Hodges?!" He was still trying to make sense of his brother.

"Wait," said Tessa, rewinding their conversation in her head. "You *made* The Great Invention?"

"Oh my no," said the professor. "That would be Gloria, the Inventor, herself."

"Wait — *Gloria?*" Gus leaned back in his chair and looked hard at the professor. "Gloria? I've heard about her, Gloria, the Inventor. My mom used to tell me stories about her when I was falling asleep. But they were just bedtime stories. Right?"

"Gloria made all of this," Professor Henchworth said gesturing around them. "I know it must sound surprising, but listen carefully. This is the most important part."

Suddenly, the ground shook, rattling the teacups on their table and vibrating their chairs.

"Is that an earthquake?" Gus yelped, gripping the edge of the table.

"Like I said," continued the professor yelling over the commotion, "there is great instability! I must tell you of the danger before our time is up! Just as my inventions have eyepieces, The Great Invention has a single eyepiece called the Ultimate Vider."

The rumbling calmed and quieted. Hodges pushed the hair back from his eyes. The professor continued, "There are many other viders passed around the earth, but there's only one that belongs to The Great Invention. It is the power source that sustains this Age of Heart-Sight, and the machine can only run so long without it."

"Without it?" Gus asked.

"Yes. The Ultimate Vider has been stolen, and if our time runs out, well…"

Tessa saw Hodges's face darken with understanding. She looked from one of them to the other. "Without it, *what*?" she demanded.

"Well, if The Great Invention stops working, which it will if the Ultimate Vider is not replaced soon, love will cease to exist. And so will the Wholehearteds of the world."

This took a minute for Tessa to understand. "Wait, you mean *you*?" asked Tessa.

"And *Hodges?*" Gus asked, turning pale.

"I'm afraid so," said the professor nodding solemnly.

"Ok, wait," said Tessa, trying to get the facts straight. "The Great Invention's vider has been *stolen*?"

"Yes," said the professor, sadly. "By a Shellstalker."

"What's a *Shellstalker*?" Tessa asked, unable to believe there was more she didn't know.

Gus still looked worriedly at Hodges.

"There's so much to tell you," said the professor, looking from face to face. The ground rumbled again in a low threat. "Quickly: the Shellstalkers are those who want us to have *only* eyesight. Allergia, whom you may have met?" His eyebrows rose in question, and the kids nodded. "She is one of them. Though not the most powerful, she's the most active in this city." The trembling grew, and the professor glanced up at the sky. "No time for the story of how, but you must know that the vider you carry *is* the Ultimate Vider from The Great Invention! The Shellstalkers want to destroy it, but they can only touch it if you give it to them. If they take it themselves, it will destroy them."

Suddenly a gust of wind nearly overturned the table, and the ground rocked. They grabbed each other as teacups and plates fell and broke.

"This is the Ultimate Vider?" Gus yelled.

"I'm afraid so," nodded the professor. "And now you have the job of returning it to The Great Invention."

"Us?! We don't know how to do that! And what about the Shellstalkers?" Tessa yelled over the noise. "Why can't you do it, Professor?"

The shaking grew so strong that the children's teeth chattered, and they gripped their chairs. But the professor's voice continued, "The Shellstalkers' greatest weapon — "

A roaring drowned out the professor's voice. The kids fell off their chairs and stumbled on the lurching ground. Tessa saw the professor pull a pencil from his pocket just as a gust of wind shattered the scene around them and silenced everything.

Tessa, Gus, and Hodges found themselves kneeling in the grass in the professor's front yard. Everything was still, and the professor, the blossoms, the vivid grass were all gone, replaced by an ordinary-looking day, where nothing at all felt ordinary.

CHAPTER 18

Gus clenched the vider in his fist. "*This* is the Ultimate," he said almost to himself. "The Ultimate." He turned to the others, his mind racing with questions. "Why didn't the professor just replace it himself when he had it if he knows where The Great Invention is? And why didn't he tell us how important this was when he gave it to us?"

"We never would have believed him," Tessa said, standing up shakily.

"It's ticking," said Hodges. He held the compass out for the others to see.

The arrows on the face of the compass had disappeared and been replaced with a smooth white face. Across it, printed in tiny formal letters, now glowed the words **UNTIL THE END OF THE ERA:**

4 Days, 6 Hours, 18 Minutes. The compass was counting down time.

"Four *days* and six *hours* to the END OF THE ERA?!" Tessa yelled.

"This is real. I can't believe this is real." Gus shook his head in bewilderment. "We have to get this back! But we don't even know where *back* is. And *Gloria*... So many things..."

Tessa ran to the professor's door and started knocking. "He has to be home!" she said, still pounding with the heavy knocker. No one answered. "Hodges, can you see a door to the Unseen anywhere?" She handed him the vider.

He shook his head.

"Ok, let's go back to that big door," Gus said. As if the fence could hear them, the hingeless door slipped open on its own, and the kids left the yard.

✳ ✳ ✳

As they arrived back at the community center, Tessa gave Hodges the vider again. "Lead the way!"

Hodges paused and shook his head. "No door."

"What! It can't have disappeared!" Tessa insisted.

"There's got to be another way in," Gus said.

Just then a jogger passed them on the other side of

the road. He wore a headband across his forehead and had a mop of hair that bounced as he ran. He flashed them a smile as he passed, and Tessa was surprised to find goose bumps rising on her arms. "Hey," she said quietly to Gus, nodding toward the man. The jogger had just reached the end of the block and was turning back toward them rather than rounding the corner. Tessa took the vider from Hodges, looked through, and grabbed Gus's arm. "Smoke!" she said urgently. "He turned to smoke!"

"He's one of them!" Gus said. "Let's get out of here!" They started to walk quickly the other way, but the jogger was already catching up.

"Hey kids!" They heard the beat of his running shoes behind them. "How ya doing?" He was getting closer.

"Uh, fine," Tessa said walking faster.

"What's that you've got there?" the jogger asked coming up alongside them, his eyes boring into the vider Tessa held.

"Oh, this? It's just our… our telescope. Looking at birds, you know," Tessa said, hurrying.

"Sounds fun. I love looking at birds," the jogger said. "Hey, I just found these in the park." He held out three crystals that caught the light and glinted in his hand. "What about a trade? Treasure for treasure!" The man reached toward them, and the air between them felt icy.

"No!" Gus yelled, and the kids broke into a run. The jogger's steps pounded right behind them.

"Let's make a trade!" His voice blew cold. He was close. Tessa felt a chill run from her neck, down the bones of her spine all the way into her legs. She pushed herself to sprint but then heard the runner's voice behind her, "Hey kid, you don't look so good." Over her shoulder she saw Gus had slowed down and was holding his side as if he had a cramp. The jogger was right beside him.

"You ok?" Tessa called. Gus nodded but seemed distracted, staring at the jogger who now spoke too quietly for Tessa to hear. *What's he saying?* As Tessa ran up, the jogger was just offering Gus his water bottle.

"It's icy cold," the man said. Gus looked dazed and reached groggily for the bottle.

"Don't!" Tessa yelled, and Hodges slapped Gus's hand, knocking the water bottle to the ground.

"Ow!" said Gus, blinking and stepping back. "I just wanted a sip." He shook his head as if he were confused.

"Hodges is right, c'mon Gus," Tessa pleaded,

looking nervously at the runner who was picking up his bottle from the ground. "We've got to get out of here."

Hodges pulled on Gus's arm, and Gus followed.

"Wait up!" the voice called from behind them.

They ran to the corner, and Tessa pushed the boys through the door of a coffee shop. She looked back to see the jogger glare at them through the glass and then turn and jog away.

CHAPTER 19

"Take it easy there, kids," the man behind the counter called, disapprovingly.

They fell into the nearest chairs. "I guess we did sprint in here," Tessa said.

"I bet if we'd run home, that guy would have kept following us. Good idea to come in here, Tess," said Gus, looking around. He seemed to be himself again.

"What happened back there?" Tessa asked.

"I don't know," Gus said. "It was like there was a magnet in my brain pulling me over to him, like I *had* to listen. As soon as he said I didn't look good, I didn't feel good. It was so weird. I couldn't think or walk away—until you knocked me, Hodges." He looked at Hodges. His face was red and sweaty. "Are you ok?"

Hodges nodded, pushing the hair back from his forehead.

"What's that from?" Gus asked, grabbing Hodges's hand. He had a red splotch on the back of his hand that was starting to blister.

"Cold," Hodges said.

"Is that from that guy's *water bottle?*" Tessa asked. Hodges nodded. "It *burned* you with cold!?"

"That's insane!" Gus frowned and flashed Tessa a concerned look. "I'll go get some ice. You sure you're ok, Hodges?"

Hodges nodded, and Gus rumpled his hair as he walked by. A minute later, Gus returned to the table with a glass of water and a large lemonade with three straws. "Good thing I still had a few dollars in here," he said patting his backpack affectionately. "And the guy at the counter said cold water's better for burns than ice." The kids sat quietly for a minute sucking down the cold, sweet drink as Hodges soaked his hand in the water cup.

Directly on the other side of the window, on the coffee shop patio, a couple sat arguing at a table. Gus picked up the vider to watch them. He saw a dart fly out of the woman's mouth as she spoke and stab the man in the arm. When he responded, a dart launched from his mouth, and stuck in the woman's shoulder. Back and forth, their words flew, lodging into each other's bodies.

"Oof!" Gus said, rubbing his own shoulder involuntarily. "Make them stop!" He gave the vider to Tessa. "I don't want to look at them anymore!"

* * *

When the kids walked outside, they saw a huge woman with short red-dyed hair sitting by herself on a bench. They'd seen her before. She was a regular in the neighborhood; she worked at the grocery store and spent all her breaks smoking on this bench. Her large face was pockmarked, and her pants were always short and too tight so her large ankles squeezed out below the cuffs. Kids on the bus called her crude names and cracked jokes when the bus passed her, and Tessa always felt a little sorry for her.

Hesitantly, Tessa lifted the vider and looked past the miserable couple with darts sticking out of their bodies, to the woman sitting alone, puffing on her cigarette. Tessa stopped and stared: inside the woman's body were flowers, not a few but hundreds of bright living flowers growing densely together. Here and there, in the middle of the flowers, Tessa noticed some bare spots, not bare earth, but flakey bare patches of skin, especially on the woman's arms and shins. They looked strange and naked surrounded by such lush flowers and made Tessa feel uncomfortable. She looked away.

Hodges had spotted the woman, too, and ran over to her before Gus could stop him.

"Hodges—" Gus started. "We don't even know her," he finished under his breath, then watched as Hodges flung himself into her arms. "What the —!"

"Hodges seems to," Tessa said, watching. "Do we actually know *anything* about Hodges?"

"I'm starting to think not." Gus watched Hodges and the woman smile at each other. She said something right in his ear, and he kissed a place on her arm before walking back over to Tessa and Gus.

"What was that about?" Gus asked with disbelief. "How do you even know her?"

"She's everywhere," said Hodges. "And I love to smell her flowers."

Gus shook his head. As they left, Tessa glanced back through the vider at the woman, and there where Hodges had kissed her, on a bare patch on her arm, something green had sprouted.

CHAPTER 20

Not knowing where else to go, the kids headed toward Gus's house. The low churning storm clouds made the evening feel later than it was. A car rolled up next to them, and an attractive woman about Mika's age rolled down her window.

"Excuse me!" she called. "Could you please tell me how to get to Key Bridge? I've gotten a bit mixed up."

Tessa, who prided herself in her knowledge of the city, felt Hodges tug the back of her t-shirt as she walked over to the car door. When she bent down toward the window, a blast of air conditioning hit her face. "Your AC feels good," Tessa said, leaning closer to give the woman directions.

"And where are *you* all going?" the woman asked. "I'd be happy to give you a ride, and help with those groceries of yours," she said, glancing at Gus.

Gus, who still held the single crumpled bag, whispered, "What shady adult offers rides to kids?" But Tessa spoke over him, spouting facts about the Potomac River and all the history she'd learned about the Key Bridge. The woman listened impatiently, giving Gus enough time to take the vider from Tessa's hand and see the driver turn to smoke.

"It's another one!" he yelled. The woman shot him a look.

"Be gone!" said Tessa backing away. "Be gone!" As the kids took off down the street, they heard the woman call after them, but they didn't stop until they reached Gus's front stoop. The woman hadn't followed them.

Gus bent over with his hands on his knees to catch his breath. Then he looked up at Tessa. "Be *gone*?" he asked, starting to laugh. "Why'd you say that to her?"

"I don't know!" Tessa said, laughter rising in her voice like relief. "That was the only thing I could think of!" Now that she'd uncorked it, the laughter kept coming until her whole body shook with it, and tears stung her eyes. "It isn't even that funny!" she said, gasping for breath.

"It *is!*" Gus said. "It's like you channeled a wizard or

something – *be gone!*" He threw his head back, laughing.

"These freaks everywhere!" Tessa gulped for air. "Are they always here?" She turned to Hodges and suddenly realized he might actually know the answer.

He nodded. "But more." He looked around. "Smoky."

Tessa looked at the cloudy sky, then picked up the vider. "Can you see the smoke without the vider?" she asked.

Hodges nodded.

Gus shook his head. "What else haven't you told us?"

Hodges shrugged. "Thought you saw, too."

They all sat for a moment wondering what to do next.

"Oh," said Hodges, interrupting the silence and pushing his hair back from his eyes. "Found this." He pulled a bright gold coin, a little bigger than a quarter, from his pocket. It glinted in his hand.

"Cool," Gus said. "Where'd you get that?"

"Michael," Hodges said shrugging.

"*Michael?* Like the guy on the corner, Michael?" Tessa frowned at Gus over Hodges's head as Hodges nodded.

110

"When did you talk to him?" Gus asked, handing Tessa the coin. It felt heavier than a quarter and had a thin ridge around the edge. Tessa had a nagging sense she'd held it before.

"Let me see it again," said Gus. He ran his finger around the small lip of the coin. "If this thing is gold, Hodges, I bet you could pawn it for a lot of money." He gently tossed it from hand to hand and then flipped it back to Tessa.

She looked closely at the smooth surface with no markings. "I think my dad has something like this on his keychain," she said, turning it over. "Actually, I think it's *just* like this, but with a hole for the key ring. I wonder where he got his?" She gave it back to Hodges.

"How'd you see Michael?" Gus asked again.

"Passed him," Hodges answered. "And he pointed."

"To the coin?"

Hodges nodded. "On the ground." Hodges looked at it again. "Great treasure," he whispered and slipped it back into his pocket.

"We've got to keep searching!" Gus said standing up.

Just then Mika pushed the door open behind them. "*There* you are!" she said. "It's late, even for a summer night!"

"What time is it?" Tessa asked, digging her phone out of her pocket. She hadn't even looked at it all day. "Woah! It's 8:30??"

Hodges nodded, and suddenly Tessa felt how hungry she was. And how tired.

Mika looked at Hodges's eyes. "This one's got to get to bed. Come on, Gus, Lucy left a little while ago, and dinner's still on the table. Tessa, I think your dad's on his way."

Tessa quickly scrolled through her unread texts and saw Mika had written an hour ago. "Sorry we didn't text you back, Mika! I forgot even to look at my phone!" Tessa knew that the one firm phone rule was to answer parents right away. "I didn't even hear it buzz," she said sheepishly.

"We'll let it slide this once, since it's the first Friday of summer," said Mika, scooping Hodges off the porch. "But it can't be a new habit." She smiled wearily.

"I promise," Tessa said.

"But we can't go to bed," Gus protested. "The professor gave us a job. We have to keep going!"

Mika looked at him. "I believe you do. But, unfortunately you've got to eat, too. And sleep, or nothing will go very well."

Gus hesitated and looked at Tessa.

"I guess," Tessa agreed reluctantly. "7:00 sharp tomorrow morning?"

"Ok! Meet you right here."

Tessa walked slowly as she scrolled through her missed texts: one from Mika, 17 from Rink sent from her mom's phone with pictures of every item Rink had tried on at the store, and one from her dad:

Loochie says she hasn't seen a trace of you!

Tessa rolled her eyes.

She left sopa negra in the fridge. I will be

home by 8:45! See you then!

Tessa's dad made a point of using real spelling and punctuation in his texts, insisting "U" wasn't a word. It made Tessa smile. She glanced again at the time — he'd be home soon!

The last unread message on her phone was from Molly! Tessa knew Molly was taking exams this week and hadn't expected to hear from her.

Hi T! Summer for you!! I'm almost done too!

Have break before internship - coming

home next Fri for weekend! loooove you!

She was coming in one week! Tessa couldn't wait. She walked into the kitchen. Fresh tostones sprinkled with salt lay on a paper towel. Tessa's mouth watered as she slipped them into the microwave and ladled black bean soup into two bowls. *Thanks, Loochie,* she thought, as the front door opened.

"I'm home!" Her dad's voice filled the house, and Tessa ran to see him. She loved the smooth feel of his work shirt against her cheek, and how his rough chin caught in her hair. He smelled like wood and dryer sheets. She took a deep breath in.

"You're home!" she said.

"*You're* home," he answered. Her mom had always said that when she hugged them. She'd told them whenever any of them were together, they were home.

Tessa squeezed her dad.

CHAPTER 21

Even at 7am, the muggy air clung to their skin. The clouds hung low and looked stormy again, though it wasn't raining. Tessa, Gus, and Hodges stood on the corner trying to decide where to go. Gus pulled a grease-stained paper towel out of his pocket. "Bacon?" he asked, unfolding it. "My dad made it."

"Always," said Tessa. Hodges took a piece too. "Maybe there's a door in the *pool?*" Tessa said, feeling sweat prickle her skin.

"Ulterior motives!" Gus called, though cooling off already sounded good, as early as it was. "Other ideas?"

"Michael's house?" Hodges asked.

Tessa and Gus exchanged glances. They knew Michael was homeless.

"Ummmm, Hodges?" Tessa said carefully. "Do you mean his *corner*? Michael doesn't have a house."

"Everyone does," said Hodges.

"Must be nice to be five," Tessa whispered to Gus.

Hodges started walking down the street ahead of them.

"Where ya goin', Hodges?" Gus asked.

"Michael's," he said again.

With no better ideas, Tessa and Gus followed him, nudging each other silently. A few blocks away, Hodges pointed to an alley where Michael leaned against the wall. "Look," Hodges said.

Tessa and Gus waved awkwardly to Michael and the row of green trashcans. "Uhhh, Hodges," Tessa whispered. "The alley?"

"House," he said again. "Look."

"Oh," said Gus uncertainly, pulling the vider from his pocket. "Through this?... Oh!" He handed the vider to Tessa. Sure enough, Michael, whom she'd just seen standing in the alley, was now brilliant white, standing in front of a small neat rowhouse with a narrow front porch. Rosy light emanated from the bricks, and he seemed to be looking at the kids expectantly. Tessa shrugged at Gus, and the three of them slowly walked over. Without the vider, Michael appeared like regular Michael again in his dirty green t-shirt. Neither Tessa nor Gus *knew* Michael and now they really didn't know what to say. Was he homeless or did he live in a glowing house?

"Bet you have questions," Michael said, in greeting. His voice was gentle and unhurried.

"Um hi, I'm Tessa." She spoke fast and gestured to the boys. "And this is Gus and Hodges." Michael smelled like he hadn't showered for days because he probably hadn't, and Tessa tried not to make a face.

"I know," Michael said nodding, a smile spreading across his face. "I know who you are." His eyes laughed, but not unkindly.

"Uh, we like your house?" Tessa fumbled, feeling awkward. His smile deepened. "And, uh, we, well, we thought you might be able to help us? We have the Ultimate Vider?" All of her words curled into questions. "If you — you might know something?"

Michael laughed a deep laugh, but Tessa could tell he wasn't making fun of her. "I sure do. Come sit," he said, settling comfortably on the ground. Tessa and Gus followed Michael's lead and sat down on the asphalt, which felt surprisingly soft under them. *Would it be a couch through the vider?* Tessa wondered.

"We're trying to find The Great Invention," Gus

jumped in. "We were talking to the professor — you know him?"

"Oh yes," said Michael.

"Ok, well, he was just starting to tell us what to do, but there was an earthquake, and he never finished what he was saying," Gus explained.

"I believe it was about the Shellstalkers," said Michael. The kids looked startled. "I was there, too," he said. "Look for me next time." His eyes twinkled. "He was telling you about Allergia and the Shellstalkers."

"Right," said Gus, looking at Michael with confusion. "And about the Ultimate, and how we have to return it! But how?"

"Good question. First let me back up," Michael said. "The Great Invention is guarded by Whole-hearteds who've devoted their entire lives to protecting it. They're the warriors among us. The professor is one." Tessa and Gus looked surprised.

"A warrior?" Gus asked. He smiled. "I can only picture the professor in his tweed coat."

"Remember, things often aren't what they seem," Michael said. Tessa thought of his mysterious alley-house. "The Wholehearteds guard with songs — day and night they sing to each other about Gloria, and the beautiful Unseen. The Shellstalkers can't come anywhere near them."

"Are they not allowed near The Great Invention?" Gus asked.

"Oh, they're allowed, but The Great Invention reveals people as they really are. The Shellstalkers have no hearts left, no true selves, they're just smoke. The Great Invention would reveal that and leave them that way for good. So they don't dare go near it."

"They would stay smoke forever?"

Michael nodded.

"But if they can't come near The Great Invention, how'd they steal the vider in the first place?"

"With their voices." Thunder growled across the sky and lighting flashed. Suddenly it was pouring.

CHAPTER 22

The kids threw their arms over their heads but were already soaked. Michael motioned them to move against the wall where the roof's overhang provided a sliver of shelter.

"Brrr!" said Tessa shaking her wet hair. "I went from sweating to goosebumps in five seconds! Ok," she said, regrouping and looking at Michael. "Go on."

The four of them huddled with their arms crossed as Michael yelled to be heard above the downpour. "The Shellstalkers' voices are their biggest weapon."

"Oh! That's what the professor must have started to say when the earthquake came!" Tessa said looking at Gus.

"That's not where I thought he was going!" said Gus. "Their voices?"

"Yes. They're relentless and persuasive. And hard to resist," Michael warned.

"Maybe that's why you wanted that jogger's water so badly?" Tessa said to Gus.

"Yeah, that was crazy — it was like I was under a spell."

"Yes," Michael continued. "You must resist them. That's what went wrong at The Great Invention — one of the Wholehearted guards started listening to Shellstalker-talk. Shellstalkers' voices can travel even where their bodies can't. The guard could hear the Shellstalkers on the wind, and she started to believe them. Most guards ignore the voices, but this particular guard tuned in. She listened and listened to them until one day she could hear *only* them."

"What were they saying to her?" Tessa asked. The rain stopped as suddenly as it had begun.

"Oh, that's better," Michael said looking around. "The Shellstalkers said, '*We need you. We need you. We need you. Come join us. Join us. Bring the vider. Get the vider.*' It was as simple as that. But listening to them made her forget her purpose. She became obsessed with joining them, and one day, she grabbed the Ultimate Vider and ran."

"She *stole* it for them?" Gus asked incredulously.

"She tried. But as she ran, the old guard songs flooded back into her memory. She became conflicted and slowed down. Ultimately, she couldn't let herself betray The Great Invention completely, and she collapsed."

"Then what happened?"

"Gloria got her," Michael said.

"Killed her?" asked Gus.

"Oh, no!" Michael laughed. "Gloria brought her back and took care of her until she grew whole again."

"But what about the Ultimate? Gloria didn't just put it back on her own invention?"

"She couldn't. None of us can. Once the Ultimate's been taken, it can only be replaced by a child. That was part of Gloria's original design to keep it pure. That's why she gave it to the professor."

"The professor knew all the time that he had the Ultimate!" Tessa exclaimed. Somehow, she'd assumed he'd just learned it himself.

"Yes. And that's where you enter the story." Michael looked at them kindly and paused.

"But why *us*? We don't know anything about this stuff!" Tessa protested.

"You have a bloodline of Wholehearteds. Both of you do," Michael said.

A bloodline? Tessa wondered. *Ok, Hodges, yes, that could make sense. But did* she *have a bloodline too?*

The kids heard someone and turned to see Mika hurrying over.

"Mom! What are you doing here?" Gus asked, surprised.

"Hi," she said, breathing hard and smiling at Michael. "I knew you didn't have umbrellas, so I came to find you."

"You never do stuff like that," Gus said, eyeing her suspiciously.

"I know," she said, smiling. "Just making sure you're all right! There's a lot happening." She handed Michael a bundle that looked like a towel and a fresh t-shirt.

"Thanks, Mika," he said. "You all get dry. I'll see you again soon." He nodded a goodbye and strolled out of the alley.

"You know *him*, too?" Tessa asked.

Mika nodded. "Yeah, for a long time."

Tessa shook her head. She was hardly even surprised.

"Shellstalkers," Hodges said, taking his mom's hand.

Mika nodded with a flicker of understanding. "Why don't you all dash home and put on dry shirts before

123

you go."

Tessa noticed Mika didn't ask them to stay or ask where they were going.

Gus noticed, too. "Mom," he said slowing to a stop. "You know what's going on, don't you? Michael just said something about bloodlines." He hesitated. "Are you…" He studied her familiar face for a second longer. "Are you Wholehearted?" Tessa's chest pounded as she waited for the answer.

Mika looked at each of them. "Yes," she said with a firm nod. "I am."

"My head is exploding!" Gus yelled with a goofy look of wonder on his face.

"We've got a lot to catch up on," Mika said.

Just then, Hodges's compass started glowing as if a lightbulb were inside of it.

"Did anyone know the compass could do *that*?" Gus asked. "What's it say, Hodges?"

"3 Days, 10 Hours, 22 Minutes," Hodges read.

Mika started walking again, quickly. "You have to hurry!" Then she looked at them with a smile as warm as sunlight. "I'm proud of you three, you know."

CHAPTER 23

As she unlocked her front door, Tessa's mind rumbled through the last ten minutes: *Michael's house. Shellstalkers' voices. Only kids for the Ultimate. And Mika, Wholehearted! Michael had said they* both *had Wholehearteds — who did he mean?*

Tessa dug through her drawers of unfolded clothes and pulled out a tanktop, hesitated and grabbed a long sleeve, too. When she came downstairs she heard the boys clamor into the kitchen through the backdoor.

"My mom sent these," Gus said, holding a stack of peanut butter and banana sandwiches. "Since somehow it's already 2:15!"

"Time's weird," said Tessa turning around to get napkins from the stack on the counter. "But your *mom*," Tessa said meaningfully.

"I know," Gus said, shaking his head like he couldn't believe it either. "How could she not have told us?" Tessa thought he sounded more in awe than betrayed. But why *hadn't* Mika told them? A small ribbon of anger uncurled inside of Tessa. She'd always trusted Mika. Tessa pushed the feeling away, picked up the note her dad had left this morning and read it to herself:

Morning early bird!
You were gone even before my early meeting. Will be back
to get my things before I go to New York tonight.
Love you!
Dad

"Oh right," said Tessa. "I forgot he has that meeting-thing in New York today." She flipped the paper over and wrote back. Kitchen notes were a thing her mom had started. Tessa still had a box of notes she'd saved, and she pulled them out now and then to look at her mom's familiar loopy script. There was no real reason to leave notes anymore since she, Cassie, and her dad could text, but they still did for old time's sake.

Hi Dad!
With Gus and Hodges. Will miss you in NYC!
Love you! XO

She scribbled the note and left it on the counter.

"Where to?" Gus asked.

"Good question. Michael didn't even give us a clue!" Tessa said. "I guess we could go to the professor's house. Maybe he's back?"

Within a few minutes they stood facing the wall-like fence. "Open fence!" Gus commanded, pushing the slats. "I think this is where the door was."

Tessa banged with the heel of her hand. "Professor? Are you home?" she called.

"A little help, Hodges?" Gus said. Hodges was standing looking at the sky. Just then the alley rang with a buzzing noise.

"ACK!" Tessa yelled, ducking. It sounded like a swarm of bees. The sound grew louder and black lines slashed through the very air in front of them. Tessa screamed, and all three jumped back. Gus reflexively threw his arm in front of Hodges.

In a second, a black rectangle hung above the kids, who cringed on the pavement. The professor's head popped into view and then his whole body. He was holding yellow pencils.

"Did your pencils do that?" Gus asked looking at

the gaping hole in the air.

"Indeed," the professor said, tucking the pencils into his chest pocket and climbing into the alley. The black glittering hole faded behind him.

"The *pencils*!" Tessa said, beaming at Gus. They'd wondered about those.

"*How?*" asked Gus, still looking at the space where the opening had been.

"As I've said, the Seen and Unseen are always both present," the professor said, straightening his jacket. "Some of us move more easily between them!"

"I don't even know what that means," Tessa muttered.

"Professor, we don't know how to get to The Great Invention," Gus said.

"That is precisely why I'm here," he nodded knowingly. "But first, there is more to tell you — come this way." Instantly the door in the fence opened, and the children followed him into the yard.

The inventions looked brighter and more whimsical than before, and Tessa and Gus couldn't help but pause and let their eyes climb over the tubes and tunnels.

Hodges giggled and ran straight to a low invention made of springy tumbling tunnels. He kicked a red handball into one and watched it ricochet and bounce, disappearing into a hole with a cartoon-like boinging sound that made an eyepiece pop out at the other end. He galloped over and looked in. "A baby one!" he squealed. "Packasindrias!"

The professor laid his hand on the top of Hodges's head. "Unfortunately, we don't have time for inventions today. Come along."

* ✳ *

Entering the professor's house, Tessa stopped to make sure they'd followed him through the same door as they had other day. Indeed they had, but today the cozy eating area looked completely different. Instead of soft florals, the room was painted a bold blue from top to bottom. There were purple striped curtains, a loud paisley tablecloth, and green plaid cushions. This time, the table was set for four with steaming tea and small bowls of pudding already dished up. Tessa hoped this would become a regular snack stop.

The professor settled into an armchair by the window. "Nothing like a little pudding to brighten the spirits," he said, scooping up a bite. "Butterscotch, my favorite!" His eyes twinkled. "Now, down to business, my friends. There's one Shellstalker we haven't discussed yet, the most powerful of all of them."

Tessa shivered thinking about someone creepier than Allergia.

"His name is Bronken, and he will do just about anything to get the vider you are holding."

Hodges's compass lit up and glowed hotly on his chest again. "Ouch," he said, holding it away from his body with the string.

"Ahh, reminders," the professor said approvingly. "Oh!" his forehead furrowed, and he squinted through the windows behind them. "Time is short, indeed." They spun around to see dense near-black thunderheads gathering low in the sky. An icy wind blew in through the screen, and goosebumps ran up the children's arms.

"I'm so sorry to leave abruptly," the professor said jumping up. "I'm needed!" Before they could ask another question, he slashed a door in the air with his pencils and dove through.

"What about us?" Gus called, but the opening glittered and faded away.

Hodges, Tessa, and Gus still sat at the table staring at the empty chair in the quiet kitchen.

"He's gone. Why didn't he take us?!" Tessa asked with frustration.

Gus noticed Hodges looked pale. "What's up, buddy?"

"Dark." Hodges's voice came out small, and he kept looking past Tessa out the window.

"The sky?"

Hodges nodded. "Air."

Tessa and Gus followed his gaze. "What do you see, Hodges?" Tessa asked, craning her neck to see the clouds better.

"Shellstalkers."

Gus shivered as he watched the dark clouds blowing. "It's ok, Hodges," he said, despite his own doubts. "We're going to find the professor and The Great Invention."

"What does the professor *do* when he's there?" Tessa wondered aloud.

"And where, exactly is *there* because *there* is supposed to be *here*, right? But there are doors?" Gus rubbed his temples.

"He sings," Hodges said.

No one spoke for a minute.

"Sings?" Tessa asked blankly.

Hodges nodded. "To the Wholehearteds. Leads the guards."

"How do you know that?" Gus asked quietly.

"Saw him," Hodges said.

Gus's mouth fell open but before he could ask more, Tessa cut in. "Did you see the look on the professor's face before he left? He looked really worried."

"Yeah," said Gus getting up from the table. "We should hurry and go — somewhere?" He gave a half laugh as he pushed open the door. "We've gotta try, right?"

A shiver ran up Tessa's back as she looked at the stormy sky and thought of unseen Shellstalkers lurking above her.

CHAPTER 24

Air much too chilly for June blew through their t-shirts. Tessa pulled on her long sleeve. It didn't rain again, but it felt like it would all afternoon. After an hour of walking around and looking through the vider, they still hadn't found anything.

"This isn't working!" Tessa said, her face pale in the storm-light. "Even Hodges hasn't seen a door! Why didn't the professor just take us — Hey!" she said as a new thought crossed her mind. "Do you think your mom could know something?"

"I don't know," Gus said, frowning. "Wouldn't she have told us?"

"She didn't before — Uh-oh." Tessa stopped walking. Allergia and two other adults were coming straight toward them.

"Well, hello," purred Allergia. In the low stormy light, her blue eyes dazzled with color. Her skin was like marble. The woman beside her was equally mesmerizing with her long dark wavy hair and high cheekbones. Her skin seemed to glow, too, as she brushed her hair back over her shoulder. Despite herself, Tessa stood transfixed. A man with a strong jaw and smooth face walked toward them, and the air cooled suddenly. Tessa pulled her hands into her sleeves and glanced at Gus who seemed equally spellbound by their beauty. Hodges slipped behind his brother.

"Are you three lost?" Allergia said with false concern.

"No," said Tessa defiantly. She felt like she could almost see her breath in the cold, though she knew that was crazy. She heard Hodges's small voice behind her whisper the word "smoky."

"It's about that vider, isn't it?" asked the man, speaking for the first time. The weight of his voice filled the alley. They were surprised to hear him use the word so freely. The other Shellstalkers they'd met seemed to avoid naming the vider at all. "We'd love the vider to be restored as well."

Tessa paused, waiting for the catch.

"Though I don't know why you're so eager to help Henchworth," the man said, his deep voice settling over them not altogether uncomfortably. "He's creative — I'll give him that — but he's desperate." Tessa had thought the man's eyes looked hard and stony but as she studied them, his eyes seemed to warm and deepen.

"Desperate?" Tessa asked, fidgeting under his gaze.

"Oh, you know, trying to get you to steal from me for his machine."

"Steal from *you*?" Gus shot back.

"This will probably be a surprise to you, but viders are *my* invention, a small way to see more. In all of Henchworth's creating, he's never been able to make a lens quite like mine." The man read the surprise on the kids' faces. "That's not what he told you, is it? And he probably didn't tell you who I am, either."

The kids looked skeptically at him, and no one responded.

"Let's start again properly. I'm Bronken, the inventor of the vider."

Tessa caught her breath — Bronken.

"You didn't *invent* viders," Gus spat.

Bronken smiled. "Let me start from the beginning. Henchworth and I have known each other since we were kids; we grew up together. Did he tell you that?"

Grew up together? Tessa had never thought of the professor as a boy before — and with Bronken?

"When we were younger, we constantly strove to outdo each other! He could outdo almost anyone — he's brilliant! — which is why we made such a powerful team working together all those years."

"Working together?" Tessa asked. This wasn't making any sense.

"He seems to have left lots of holes in his story," Bronken said, raising his eyebrows. "Let me fill you in: as young men, Henchworth and I worked together for the government, building surveillance equipment. I can't go into specifics, of course, but together, and separately, we've built countless devices and invented the most cutting-edge espionage equipment."

"You worked together for the CIA?" Tessa asked. She'd done an in-depth report last year on the CIA for school and learned spying wasn't just in the movies; undercover agents sworn to secrecy really did have all sorts of spy devices and travel all over the world.

"I don't believe you," Gus said. "The professor's never said anything about spying or the government."

"That's why we live here, in Washington, D.C. Most of our work was through the Pentagon. Henchworth became an expert making tools of illusion, and I made the lenses. Together we created extremely powerful machines used in all different areas of defense. That was years ago, now. Before the professor *changed*."

Tessa didn't like how he'd said "changed," like it was awful.

"*Changed?*" Gus challenged, his fists tight.

"Well, when he was still a young man, oh, about 20 years ago, he went funny. I don't know what else to call it, as if he'd hit his head, though there was no accident that I know of. He began confusing what was real and what was not. He latched on to an old mythology and began talking nonsense about an Unseen world. He was obsessed! Pretty quickly, he lost his job and became secluded. I didn't hear anything about him for years.

"But then he began to lure in children. That's when it got serious, and I became involved. He's done this before, you know. It's his scheme — he ropes kids in through stories and puts them up to all kinds of dirty work. It's not safe. He has to be stopped."

Tessa glanced quickly at Gus.

"That's not true," said Gus, color rising to his face. "The professor's not *crazy*."

"Is he not?" asked Bronken.

"And the lens isn't yours!" said Gus, instinctively putting his hand over his pocket. "It belongs to The Great Invention."

"Mmm, The Great Invention," said Bronken. "That's all part of his game. I bet he's told you about a wonderful inventor named Gloria who holds the world together?" His tone cut sarcastically, and Tessa's heartrate quickened. "It's a good story," Bronken continued. "I'll give him that. But that's all it is. There *is* no Great Inventor. How could there be? It's nonsense. Think about it: An inventor whose one, unseen machine affects the consciousness of *all* people on the earth over *all* time? It's an *impossible* thought!"

It *did* sound ridiculous when he said it that way, Tessa thought. Her cheeks got hot, and she was sure they were turning red. "But," she pressed, "he couldn't have made everything up — what about the compass, and the doorway, and how everyone looks?" Her mind raced through the last week.

"It's obviously real!" Gus almost shouted.

Bronken sighed. "No doubt the man is *clever,* the way he uses toys. Let me see that compass." He reached out, and Hodges slinked further behind Gus.

"Leave us alone," Gus snarled.

Bronken laughed. "Don't worry, Gus. We're just having a conversation. Henchworth isn't a *bad* guy, don't get me wrong, but as I said, he's confused, not mentally sound. You need to protect yourselves and recognize what's happening. Henchworth still has a few of the viders we used together — they're beautiful little creations, with illusional elements. He's given you one of those."

Gus took a step back, his hand still on his pocket.

"Every so often Henchworth picks kids to go on these missions," Bronken used air quotes around missions. Tessa hated when adults did that. "He preys on kids because adults would never believe him. You'll see the adults he ropes in to help him aren't what I'd call the most dependable. Homeless men, in particular."

Tessa's stomach clenched.

"But," said Gus in a low voice, "we've seen real stuff through the vider."

Bronken took a deep breath. "Gus, think of all the magicians over time — Houdini, David Copperfield, David Blaine — each seemed undeniably magical, but each was simply a master of illusion."

This sudden possibility jarred Tessa. Magicians had always intrigued her. She loved trying to figure out their moves and spot weaknesses in their acts. Bronken was right; those masters were flawless. Could the vider really be a magic trick, too?

"Henchworth is a master of illusions. He can impose scenery so it looks like our daily world transforms, he can —"

"We haven't just seen *scenery* and *projections*," Gus cut in. "We've seen *real* people and *real* places."

Tessa didn't like the uncertainty growing in her as Bronken continued.

"He'd like you to think that." Bronken's face showed pity. "That I'm only smoke and mirrors, out to get you, of all things. Do I look like smoke?" Bronken slapped his hands against his legs, clapped his hands. "Pretty solid to me," he said, smiling. "The saddest part is that Henchworth believes everything he's telling you. That makes him especially dangerous. We just don't know *how* dangerous. He's never kidnapped anyone, yet." Tessa jumped at the word, and Bronken continued. "We've intercepted him every time. We're not sure that's even his intention, but let's not find out." Bronken smiled softly. "Think it all over," he continued. "Decide for yourselves what makes sense."

What if what Bronken was saying *did* make sense?

Tessa's face burned.

"Henchworth lives in his own little world that he's the center of." Bronken's eyes filled with concern. "Think about it — he lives in your neighborhood. Has he ever shown an inkling of care for anyone else?"

Tessa couldn't think of ever having seen the professor with anyone else. She couldn't see Hodges nod as he stood behind Gus.

"Do you have any reason to believe what he says is true, that he's actually laboring for the greater good?"

"My mom—" Gus began.

"Yes, we've talked to your mom," he said, nodding at Gus. "We want to work together to protect you." He turned again to Tessa. "Magic tricks aren't enough to put stake in." Bronken's eyes shone clear and bright. "Think about it. I'm here to help." He handed Tessa a shiny black business card. She looked down at the name printed in firm gold letters: BRONKEN, with his phone number neatly underneath. When she looked back up, the Shellstalkers, if that's what they were, had left.

CHAPTER 25

Tessa turned the slippery card over in her fingers.

"He did *not* talk to my mom! I don't believe *any* of that!" Gus fumed. "Let's throw that thing away," he said, gesturing toward the card. "I wish we could burn it!"

"I don't know," said Tessa. Her head swam with Bronken's words.

"Trash it!" Gus said with disgust, pointing at a big green trashcan they were passing. As Tessa opened the can and was about to toss the smooth black card, she felt a twinge of uncertainty. Gus and Hodges were a step in front of her and didn't see her slip the card into her pocket and slam the trashcan lid closed.

"But Gus," Tessa said. "What if he's right? What if the professor's *crazy?*"

"He *isn't*. We know him. This stuff is real!"

"I know, but… We don't know him *that* well. What if he really *is* just a master of illusion, of virtual reality that *feels* real?"

"Tessa, you can't believe them! That's just what they want."

"But Gus, what if we're wrong! What if we're making fools of ourselves, and the professor's using us for some weird plan?"

"He *isn't*. What would that plan even *be?*" Gus demanded.

"I don't know. I don't know what to believe." Tessa started walking fast.

"Wait up!" Gus said hurrying after her.

A car pulled up alongside them, honking, and glided to the curb.

"Rink!" Tessa yelled, running over to the car. "I'm *so* glad to see you!" Tessa was surprised how relieved she felt to see someone other than Gus.

Rink laughed. "We've only been out of school a few days!"

"Hi Mrs. Trolly," Tessa said.

"Hey Trollys," she heard Gus call from behind her.

"School seems like ages ago!" Tessa said, sounding dramatic but meaning it.

"How's summer so far?" Rink asked. If only Tessa had time to explain. Rink would love to sink her teeth into *this* weirdness. "Oh!" said Rink, interrupting her own question. "Have you checked your phone? I've been texting you all morning!" Tessa shook her head. Rink was almost bouncing. "I ran into Maggie from Mrs. Well's homeroom, and she said — wait for it! — Samantha and her mom are *moving* to *Tennessee* this summer – can you believe it?! Her mom got custody and they're leaving! A school without Samantha Shaw?"

A huge weight seemed to vaporize from Tessa's shoulders. She could hardly imagine a school day without Samantha tormenting her, and now she'd have all of seventh grade to herself! Delight danced across Rink's face, too.

"We've gotta go," said Mrs. Trolly, smiling apologetically at Tessa.

"She's making me check out a summer reading book. I know —" Rink rolled her eyes. "That sounds fun to you." She smiled. "Send me packages at camp!"

"I always do!" Tessa said, hugging Rink through the car window.

"Dosvedanya!"

"Dosvedanya!" Tessa called as the car pulled away.

"No Samantha!" Gus said, leaning to give Tessa a high five. "That's insane!"

Tessa slapped his hand and instantly felt her surge of happiness collapse. What was her problem? This was the best news she'd heard in ages, but instead of elation, she felt annoyed that Gus was so happy. Without meaning to, she thought of Samantha stuffed with wadded papers and felt a jolt of sadness that Samantha had to live anywhere with that mom.

"Well, let's go," said Gus, starting to walk again.

A dark wave of doubt crashed over Tessa as she remembered the conversation they'd just been having. "I'm going to take a break," she said abruptly.

Gus stopped. "A break? What do you mean?"

"Yeah. I need to do some stuff," Tessa said. "I haven't even gone through my backpack or anything."

"Are you serious?!" He looked at her like she'd just grown another head.

"Yeah." She nodded defiantly.

"Your backpack?" he asked in disbelief. "We don't have time!"

"I do."

"What's the matter with you?"

"Nothing, ok? Nothing! I'm just going home for a while."

"Going home?" Gus looked stunned, but Tessa kept walking. He and Tessa never fought, and when they argued it was only ever about small things like whether the capital of Idaho was Boise or Boynton — and they always ended up laughing. But Tessa wasn't laughing.

"Is she's really leaving?" Tessa heard Gus say behind her. "How can she leave?"

"She has a shadow," Hodges said. Tessa walked even faster and didn't turn around.

CHAPTER 26

Tessa couldn't say exactly why she'd stormed off, but now she just wanted to get home.

Pushing open her front door, Tessa found Cassie lounging on the couch paging through magazines. She still wore her hat from the diner where she was working for the summer.

"Where've you been?" Cassie asked.

"Nowhere," snapped Tessa.

"Woah — what's with the mood?"

Tessa didn't answer but stalked up to her room. Why *was* she in such a bad mood? She closed the door and locked it, as if someone were about to barge in, and plunked down on the floor. She dragged her hulking backpack onto her lap and set right to work pulling books out and stacking them on the shelves.

There were notes from Rink all over the place folded in origami shapes: a box, a crane, an elephant, a cat's face. She lined them up along the windowsill. It felt good to be busy. Her zipper pouch bulged with pens, double-sided highlighters, animal-shaped erasers, and stubby pencils, some of which had teeth marks in them. She'd tried to break her pencil-biting habit, but she still secretly loved sinking her teeth into the wood. She shoved the pouch into her desk drawer.

With all the adrenaline pumping through her body the last couple of days, Tessa hadn't noticed how exhausted she was. Now in the quiet of her room, with the sky darkening outside her window, she felt the heaviness of her eyelids. Even her arms felt heavy as she unloaded the rest of her papers and notebooks from her backpack. Tessa stretched out on her bed for a minute and before she knew it, was asleep.

✳ ✳ ✳

Tessa stood in a great hall, ornate with tall pointed windows and soaring ceilings. The Great Invention was there. It looked like a giant pipe organ with silver and gold pipes reaching to the ceiling. The professor sat in front of it. He played the great instrument passionately, moving his body with the melody that leapt into the room. Just then, Bronken, wearing a smooth black suit, strode in from nowhere. He marched to the back of the room and clicked off a projector. Both the professor and the invention vanished.

"See!" Bronken yelled. "It's an illusion!" A crowd appeared behind Tessa, and the whole room roared with laughter and applause. Bronken bowed, then looked straight at Tessa, zooming close enough that his face was all she could see. "What are you waiting for, Tessa?"

✳ ✳ ✳

Tessa woke with a jolt and sat straight up, her heart pounding so hard she had to catch her breath. She swung her feet to the floor. Though her blinds were closed, she could tell the sun was already bright. She looked at the clock. It was 8:45 in the morning! She'd fallen asleep without dinner.

Bronken's shiny black business card sat like a punctuation mark on the white desk across from her bed. She picked it up. Though it was only a card, it felt cool, like it were an actual slice of obsidian. *What are you waiting for?* Bronken's question from her dream echoed around her room. Maybe he did want to help. What *was* she waiting for? His number was printed in neat square font at the bottom of the card.

She picked up her phone. No missed calls. It was

almost 9am and Gus wasn't even looking for her. Tessa looked again at Bronken's number, then dialed.

Before the phone even rang, a voice answered. "Good morning, Tessa!" Bronken sounded warm and welcoming and not at all surprised to hear from her.

"Oh, uh, hi- Mr. uh—" Tessa faltered. She hadn't expected him to recognize her number, and suddenly realized she didn't know what to call him.

The voice laughed kindly. "Call me Bronken, Tessa. I'm so glad you called! I'm just sitting down at Black Coffee about to order a breakfast burrito. Why don't you come join me!"

Tessa didn't answer. Was that weird, going to meet a strange man for burritos? But Black Coffee *was* a public place, and it was right up the street. That seemed safe. She thought about their warm cheesy burritos and then about the cold bowl of cheerios waiting for her downstairs. "Ok," she said. "Yeah, I'll come."

"Wonderful!" he said, with almost a laugh in his voice.

CHAPTER 27

Tessa wore jean shorts and a t-shirt that said *Be Kind or Go Home*. She started to kick a rock, thought of Gus, and stopped. *What am I going to say when I get there?* she wondered. *What would Gus say if he knew I were meeting Bronken?* A small sense of dread settled in her stomach. *No,* she shook her head pushing the thought away. *No, it's ok. I just want to learn what's true.*

She pushed open the coffee shop door and saw Bronken at a table in the back, reading a newspaper. Tessa paused, feeling suddenly awkward. But before she could back out the door, Bronken looked up and waved.

Tessa slid into the empty chair across from him and within seconds, burritos arrived alongside two glasses of orange juice. "Thanks," she said, surprised. "This is what my dad and I get when we come here." *Did he know that's what we always order?*

Bronken nodded, taking a sip of his coffee, and Tessa couldn't tell if this meant he had known or was just listening to her.

"Where's the rest of your crew?" Bronken asked.

Tessa's eyes dropped to the table. "Oh. They — well, they didn't come with me. I'm actually not sure what they're doing right now." Her voice strained as she tried to sound casual, glancing up at the high black ceiling.

Bronken raised his eyebrows, and when she didn't elaborate he leaned in, as if to tell her a secret. "I want to make sure you're safe," he said. His gaze was intense.

Tessa half-nodded. "I don't have the vider. Gus has it," she said all at once, realizing she'd been worried Bronken would be angry she hadn't brought it.

But Bronken looked neither surprised nor bothered. "It was brave of you to come," he said.

Tessa took a bite of her burrito. As the warm potatoes, cheese, and bacon filled her mouth, she felt herself relax a bit.

"Leaving them must have been hard," Bronken continued. "You all are good friends."

It *had* been hard to leave with Gus calling after her, and it felt good to have Bronken acknowledge that. "Yeah. They wanted to stay and find a door," Tessa said sighing. "But I needed some space. I want to know what's true, you know?"

"And I think you do know," Bronken said. "That's why you're here. For you, the line between fact and fiction is clear."

Tessa sat up a little straighter. "I just don't want to be gullible."

He smiled. "No one does. Keeping things black and white, fact and fiction, keeps life simple. It keeps our minds clear. Not everyone understands that, Tessa."

She nodded. She liked the idea of a clear mind. She understood that.

"It can be embarrassing to admit we were wrong, and it sounds like Gus wasn't quite ready to do that."

"I guess not." She frowned.

Bronken nodded in a knowing way.

"I think they're..." Tessa searched for how to say it.

"Off to find The Great Invention, right?" It sounded childish when Bronken said it. Tessa nodded. "Don't worry, Mika is keeping an eye on them."

"She is?" Tessa asked eagerly. If he'd really involved Mika, they were all going to be ok.

"Yes," Bronken said reassuringly. "And I'm glad you're here with me. Tell me more about yourself, Tessa. It's not so often I get to have breakfast with such a bright 12-year-old." Within minutes they were talking about school, clubs, and the softball team. "My niece is your same age," Bronken said, "and she loves rock climbing."

"Oh, Gus loves that too!" Tessa said. "He's in the rock climbing club at school. Next year he'll be on the team and compete against other schools. He can climb anything. Except when he freezes," said Tessa, "but that hardly ever happens. I think it only happened once, really. Hodges is learning, too. He's pretty good."

"What do you mean freezes?" Bronken asked with concern.

"Oh, well once after his grandparents' car accident, he had a meet, and in the middle of climbing, he froze." She found herself talking fast and the story poured out easily. "He couldn't climb at all. He told me later he'd started thinking about the accident and losing someone in his family, and he panicked. He couldn't even move his fingers. It was pretty bad." For a second Bronken's expression looked almost hungry, and a surge of protectiveness made Tessa add, "But he's fine now." She gave a quick reassuring smile.

Bronken's face instantly softened. "Wow, sounds like he's had some hard things happen."

"Yeah. But he's ok, really," Tessa said, eager to change the subject. She looked down at the last few bites of burrito on her plate.

"Full?" he asked.

"So full," Tessa said smiling. "Thanks for breakfast. It was so good."

"Anytime," he said.

Tessa started to get up but hesitated. "Bronken, could I ask you one more question?"

"Of course — anything! That's why we're here."

"Well," Tessa wondered how to start. "You said before that the professor became confused, that he started believing old myths and kind of went crazy. But he didn't make the stuff up, right?" Tessa searched for the right words. "I mean, the myths already existed, and there are other people who believe them, right? I'm pretty sure Mika does. So, are they all crazy or could some of it *be* true?" The question had been nagging at Tessa.

"There's believing and *believing*," Bronken said, chuckling as if it were funny. "People throw their passions into all sorts of things. I just heard about a

155

man who insists there's no gravity."

Tessa rolled her eyes. "It's like the people who say the world is flat!"

"Exactly," said Bronken, leading them out the door. "There's one in every crowd! Thanks for joining me for breakfast this morning, Tessa. I thoroughly enjoyed it." He paused and put his hand on her shoulder. "Stay safe. You know how to reach me if you need anything."

"Bye, thanks for the burrito!"

Bronken walked across the street to his black car, and as he got in Tessa noticed the windows were tinted so dark that she couldn't see him at all. She waved to the black glass.

As he drove off, she realized he really hadn't answered her question.

CHAPTER 28

Tessa's phone vibrated. "Tessa!" Rink's voice yelled. "It's my last morning, and it's finally sunny! Want to meet at the pool?"

"Yes!" Tessa felt a gush of gratitude for suddenly having a plan for her day. "I'll grab my bathing suit and meet you there!"

All day, Tessa and Rink practiced their dives and made plans for care packages and seventh grade without Samantha Shaw. During adult swim, they sucked bombpops till their lips and teeth were blue.

"It's the weirdest thing," Tessa began. "Gus and I met Professor Henchworth —"

"You've always wondered about that guy!" Rink said. "He's on the mystery list. I've only ever seen him at the hardware store and in your alley. Did you figure out what he does with all that weird stuff he buys?"

'Yeah, he's kind of… strange," said Tessa, looking for words. "He makes all these inventions in his yard —"

"So *that's* what's behind the fence!" Rink said triumphantly.

Tessa gave a weak smile. "Yeah. But he might be certifiably crazy, or at least on the legit-crazy spectrum. He claims there's an unseen world around us. I dunno…" Tessa shrugged, trying to act like she didn't care. "Gus seems to buy it."

Rink thought for a minute. "I guess you could say a lot of people think that." Tessa looked over at her questioningly. "I mean if you think about it — isn't imagination an unseen world? And love? You could even say molecules are a whole invisible world."

Tessa frowned. "I guess. I hadn't really thought about it that way." She felt grumpy, despite herself, that Rink had spun the Unseen in a positive way. She'd been looking for an ally to be skeptical with her.

"I was just reading an article about the multiverse — now that'll make your mind bend!" Rink continued. "Talk about worlds we can't see!" She kept talking, but Tessa had stopped listening. She was thinking about imagination being an unseen world as she watched the clouds drift grey and downy across the sun. Could she and Gus have somehow *imagined* the Unseen world because they'd wanted it to be there?

"HA!" Rink's voice startled Tessa and her eyes popped open. "You fell asleep! And I was telling you so much good stuff."

Tessa looked around, confused.

"It's adult swim, and I'm starved," Rink said.

"Adult swim again?"

"Yeah, you slept half an hour!" Tessa sat up. "My dad just called and is taking burgers off the grill," Rink said. "Want to come over?"

Tessa's sleep had been deep and full of dreams again. *Something had been wrong with Gus and Hodges. But a bird had come, a huge white bird.* The image flickered through Tessa's mind and disappeared. *What had the bird done?*

"Tessa?" asked Rink, leaning toward her. "You in there?"

"Yeah, sorry," said Tessa, shaking her head. She forced a smile and picked up her soggy towel, noticing with annoyance that her heart was still beating fast from her dream. *Gus had been terrified. And what had happened?* She wondered if somehow he could know about her breakfast with Bronken. She shoved the thoughts away and turned to Rink. "I'd love to come over!"

As they walked, their wet bathing suits soaking through their shorts, Rink told Tessa about the new archery course at camp and how this year she was determined to earn her master's badge. Tessa half-listened as she pictured the huge white bird from her dream, its wings spread out. It had somehow been protecting Gus...

As they passed a café, Tessa spotted something black on one of the patio tables closest to the side-walk. Instantly she knew it was Bronken's card, identical to the one she had. It sat glinting like a small hello. Without thinking, Tessa swept it off the smooth metal surface.

"What's that?" Rink asked.

"Oh, just some business card. Trash, I guess," Tessa said, trying to sound casual. Rink shrugged and started talking again. Tessa looked down at the card in her hands and gasped. Quickly her eyes darted to Rink, but Rink hadn't noticed. In sharp handwriting on the back of the card it said, *T- same time, same place tomorrow?* She looked around, but Bronken was no-where to be seen.

✳ ✳ ✳

Two burgers and a movie later, Tessa hugged Rink goodbye three times, and they walked halfway to Tessa's together before Rink turned back to finish packing. Tessa didn't want Rink to leave for so long! Her chest felt achy as she continued the walk alone. For the hundredth time, Tessa slipped her hand into her pocket and felt Bronken's card. How had he known she'd pass that table? *I guess he did used to work for the CIA*, Tessa thought. The idea of his being a spy seemed a little creepy but somehow comforting at the same time. It was nice to have someone care where she was.

She pulled out the card, its weight like certainty in her hand, and texted the number as she walked.

OK CU at 9.

CHAPTER 29

"Hello?" Tessa called as she opened the front door.

No one answered. The house was dark except for a narrow shaft of light spilling from the kitchen where her sister must have left the light on. She followed it and pushed the door open, grateful for a bright room. Stuck to the fridge with a magnet was a quickly scrawled note from Cassie, reminding Tessa that their dad was still in New York and that Cassie was at the movies with Brooke but would be home later. *Right*, Tessa thought.

For a minute, she felt as empty as the house.

Tessa pushed her glass against the water dispenser in the fridge door and listened to the ice cubes rumble in the freezer. Then she carried the glass upstairs to her room. She looked around and kicked the pile of clothes she'd rescued from Lost & Found on the last day of school to the corner. *What to do?* Rink was packing with her mom and dad. Cassie was with Brooke, as usual. Gus was — well, she wasn't going to call Gus. She stuck out her tongue and snapped a picture of herself, used a sparkly filter and sent it to Molly:

So Pretty! (pretty bored).

Then Tessa flopped on her bed. She wished her dad wasn't in New York. She pulled out a beat-up copy of *The Penderwicks* from a stack of books by her bed. It was Molly's old copy, and even though Tessa had read it many times, rereading it made her feel like Molly was closer.

$$* * *$$

His heart raced as he clung to the rockface.

"Pretty big wall you've taken him up." Bronken's deep voice boomed as a lump of guilt rose in Gus's throat. Gus had already climbed high, but the cliff wall still rose far above him, and he could hardly see Hodges nearing the top.

"Imagine a fall from that height," Bronken said. Gus pictured Hodges's small body hurtling past him, and his chest tightened. Just then a shower of crumbling rock rained down

from somewhere. Gus ducked his head and squeezed his eyes shut, spitting out dust as he yelled, "Are you OK!?"

"Ok!" the voice was faint and far away, but it was Hodges's. Gus's hands were so sweaty that the rocks felt slippery as he tried pulling himself upward. He fumbled around for a place to put his foot. He felt clumsy, like his body wasn't working. "I have to get to Hodges," he said, grabbing at a rock above him.

"At least if you were right behind him, he'd fall into you if he slipped." Bronken's voice was deep and steady. "But from this far below, there is nothing you could do."

"I'm trying," said Gus, clenching his teeth. Climbing with his long lanky body and big feet suddenly felt impossible. He couldn't move. The ground lurched below him as a dizzying panic fuzzed his brain.

Bronken's voice seemed to be everywhere now, on both sides of Gus, below and above, telling Gus about two boys who'd fallen last week rock climbing. Gus's arms and fingers started to ache from gripping. Again, he tried to move his foot up the wall, but he couldn't find a ledge.

He stared at the rock two inches from his nose and tried to take a deep breath.

Bronken's voice pressed in: "You never should have brought your brother here, you know… it's dangerous… easy to fall…"

Gus tried to call to Hodges again but nothing came out of his mouth.

"...still so far to go," Bronken said. He reached above where Gus hung. Gus couldn't see what he was doing, but when Bronken moved again, a chunk of rock loosened and crashed down on Gus's hand.

Gus screamed in pain and looked down at his fingers, two of them bent at an angle now. He pulled the throbbing hand into his chest and felt himself slipping. His knees and shoulders scraped the wall as he scrambled to hold on. And then he fell.

$$* * *$$

Tessa woke up yelling. Her heart beat loudly in her ears. She peeled her cheek off the book she'd been reading and looked around. The lights were on in her room, and she was still wearing the shorts and t-shirt she'd worn home from Rink's house.

Bleary-eyed, Tessa felt around the floor for her phone. It was 8:14 in the morning already! Her alarm was set to go off in 16 minutes to meet Bronken for burritos. She glanced out the window at Gus's house but couldn't tell if any lights were on. Then she flopped back on her pillow and stared at the ceiling, replaying the dream.

Bronken had loosened that rock and hurt Gus's hand. And Gus had fallen! Even though Tessa had been Gus in the dream, she'd also somehow watched him fall and seen him land in a heap. *It wasn't real,* she assured herself. *It was a dream.* But she couldn't help picturing Gus at the bottom of the cliff. *No. Bronken couldn't have done that.* She got up and spotted Bronken's card on her desk with the sharp handwriting on the back. *It was a dream*, she told herself again, but as she brushed her teeth she couldn't shake the cold pit of fear that something had happened to Gus, and it might have been her fault.

CHAPTER 30

Cassie and her friend Brooke were still sleeping when Tessa slipped out the front door. As her stomach rumbled, she thought of the warm cheesy burrito waiting for her. She glanced at Gus's house. *I'll just check really quickly*, she thought. She picked up a pinecone and threw it at Gus's window. No answer. She could knock, but the little knot of fear in her chest was thawing now. *He's fine.* She glanced at her phone — 8:50 — it was time to go. Just then, Gus's front door opened, and Gus's dad Marcus came out, fully dressed, holding a mug.

"Thought I heard something out here. Do you have Hodges?" he asked urgently.

"Um, no," said Tessa, caught off guard. "He's not with Gus? They're not... here?" She saw him clench his jaw muscles.

"Gus is at the Emergency Room with Mika. He fell rock climbing. I don't know the details; Michael brought him home early this morning. We don't think it's serious, but he looks pretty banged up."

Tessa felt superglued to the sidewalk.

"I don't know where Hodges is," Marcus went on in a serious tone. "He didn't come home with them. Michael says he's with the professor and that they're ok. Ok, I guess, but not necessarily *safe*." Marcus's voice trailed off. "I thought you might be with him." Tessa had never seen Marcus look so worried. His face looked different without his usual smile. She squirmed.

"We kind of got separated." Tessa felt her face get hot. "Is Gus — is he going to be ok?"

Marcus nodded. "Mika called. They're still waiting. Looks like he broke a couple fingers and has lots of scrapes and bruises. But yes — thank God — he's going to be ok. They're waiting to do a scan just to make sure there's no internal bleeding. For extra precaution."

Internal bleeding — the words hung in the air.

Marcus looked at her again. "Want to come in?"

Tessa hesitated.

"We can keep company," Marcus said, and he smiled a weary smile. She started to follow him inside when her phone rang. **Bronken.** The word flashed on the screen. She wavered and then pressed decline.

✳ ✳ ✳

Tessa could see the kettle was already hot, but Marcus turned the burner on again, and within a minute it whistled. He poured the steaming water and handed Tessa a tea bag. The milk and honey were already on the counter.

"Want to talk about what happened?" Marcus asked.

Tessa watched the milk bloom white swirls in her tea. She took a big breath. "I messed up, I think." She felt hot tears sting her eyes.

Marcus waited.

"I got mad and left them. I wasn't mad *at* them, I was just mad. I didn't know what was real. So I went home. But…" She made herself keep going. "But, then I talked to Bronken — do you know who that is?" She flinched, hoping he'd say no, but he nodded gravely. Tessa took a deep breath and continued. "Well, Bronken said he was helping, trying to keep us safe. He said he'd talked to you and Mika." She looked at him hopefully.

"No," said Marcus firmly, but his eyes were soft.

"Right," Tessa groaned. "So I think it's my fault that Gus got hurt." The sentence came out as a whisper. She stared at her tea. "I think it's my fault Bronken went rock climbing with him." Her tears felt hot and dropped on the table. "And made a rock fall on his hand. I think that was because of me." She let her eyes dart to Marcus's face. She thought of Bronken waiting in Black Coffee for her right now and felt small. "I was so stupid."

"Oh Tessa," Marcus sighed and didn't say anything for a minute. Tessa fidgeted with the handle of her mug. "Bronken is powerfully persuasive. But he can't ever be trusted."

"Yeah. I'm figuring that out… How do you know him?" Tessa felt tired of surprises.

"There was a time when we could see like you're seeing. We had run-ins with Shellstalkers, too," Marcus said. "It was a long time ago, but Bronken's just the same. He doesn't age."

"He doesn't *age*?" Tessa asked with horror. "You mean, he's always been here?"

"Something like that," said Marcus grimly.

Tessa couldn't find the words to ask another

question.

"When you showed us your vider at dinner, and Mika and I saw how powerful it was, we knew it must be the Ultimate. We had so many questions, but it was already late. Then when Mika saw the compass, we knew there really was no time to talk. So we've been trusting the professor and waiting until we were all together. We know being under the professor's care is the safest place for you to be, but even with him, there's danger." Marcus sighed.

"If you knew, why didn't you say anything! You could have helped us!" Betrayal surged through Tessa's body like electricity. It felt good to feel angry rather than ashamed of herself.

Marcus nodded. "We were watching you discover the Unseen for yourselves — we'd been hoping for that since you all were little! But we had no idea how deep in you were — that happened so fast!" Marcus's voice got quiet.

The gears in Tessa's brain fought to synthesize this new information. Mika and Marcus had known the whole time about *everything*.

"And again, I'm afraid we don't have much time," Marcus said, glancing out at the low black clouds thickening. He looked back at Tessa's frowning face.

"It's ok if you're angry we didn't tell you. I think I would be, too. But we're on your side, and we want to tell you everything. But first," concern flickered across his face, "you have to find Hodges."

"Can't you?" Tessa asked. "I mean," she tried to soften her tone. "Can't you help? If you know all about the Unseen world, can't you help me find him?" She heard her own voice pleading.

"I wish I could. It doesn't work like that. Mika and I can't see the Unseen like you do anymore, even through the vider. I'll explain it all to you, but right now, you need to find Hodges. Please."

"What about Gus?" Tessa protested.

"We'll take care of him." Marcus said.

"But —" It was as if all the blood drained from Tessa's body. "I don't know where to go. I don't know what to do." Marcus stood up and walked out of the room. Tessa could hear him digging around in the closet by the door. Gus's backpack lay unzipped on the kitchen floor, and Tessa noticed his sketch-book open on the table. Marcus must have been looking through it. The page was open to a new drawing and right away, Tessa knew it was of her. In the picture, she was walking away, and even though it was only a drawing, she could tell she looked defiant.

It was when Tessa had left. Gus had again drawn the fiery flames inside her, but this time he'd rubbed pencil on top so it looked like a shadow lay over her. Had she looked like that?

"I wonder if this will help." Marcus's voice made Tessa jump, and she straightened up quickly, as if she'd been sneaking something she shouldn't have. She stood awkwardly by the table, unsure of what to do with her hands.

"This might help," Marcus said again, oblivious to Tessa's embarrassment.

"You have a *vider*?" Tessa asked, staring at the thing in his hand.

"Yep," he said handing it to her. "It isn't the Ultimate, but it's something. It hasn't been used for a while..." A shadow crossed his face.

Tessa carefully picked it up. She could tell right away it was different. It felt much lighter than the Ultimate, and it was silver instead of gold. She instantly brought it to her eye. Marcus shimmered a bit but was pretty much unchanged. He read her confusion and clarified, "It doesn't change people in the same way, but it will help you find ways in."

Tessa examined it again. "I can't believe you have this." She looked up at Marcus. "Tell Gus I'm so sorry." Her voice cracked, and she looked quickly at the floor.

"I will. Your friendship's been strong for a long time. It'll weather this. Don't worry."

She nodded but couldn't meet his eyes. "And thanks," she said. "I needed some help."

He patted her warmly on the back and walked her to the door. "Careful out there, and good luck!"

CHAPTER 31

Tessa recognized the short stout woman stepping off the bus right away.

"What are you doing out in this heat already?" Loochie scolded.

"Oh, just looking for Hodges," Tessa said, trying to sound casual. "Cassie's still asleep."

"Of course she is," Loochie said, rolling her eyes. "These teenagers."

"Dad'll be home later today," Tessa offered.

"I know. New York. So busy!" She walked off shaking her hands in disapproval.

"See ya, Loochie!" Tessa called, and the woman waved over her shoulder.

Tessa started walking with the vider held stubbornly to her eye. If there was something to find, she didn't want to miss it. This vider was clearly weaker than the other. She could only see a faint glow where Michael's house had been. She hoped that didn't mean the vider had stopped working since Marcus had last used it.

She trudged past the market and the playground, feeling a little like a pirate with a telescope as people gave her weird looks. After about 20 minutes, she started losing hope. "Where's-a-door?" she chanted to herself, scanning the streets. "Where's-a-door? Where's-a-door? Where's-a-door?" Just then, she tripped and fell hard, scraping both of her hands and knees and slamming her right elbow.

"Owww," she groaned, pushing herself up. She looked back to see what she'd fallen over. A loose brick lay next to a manhole cover. *Stupid brick!* Tessa glared at it, wondering if it could be some trap planted by a Shellstalker. But it was just a brick, even through the vider. But the manhole cover was different! There where the manhole cover had just been, was now a perfectly round hole.

No way! Tessa thought, crawling over to look in. It was pitch black. *This has to be a door!* Without letting herself think too much about it, Tessa lowered herself down and dropped into the blackness.

The darkness lasted only a second before Tessa

landed in a sunny wood she'd never seen before. The air smelled so fresh and green, she knew this must be the Unseen. For a split second, she could see the busy street she'd just left shimmering through the smooth-trunked trees, but then it was gone. Tessa stood in the middle of a thicket with no path anywhere. Her knees stung and elbow ached from her fall.

"Hodges?" she shouted, looking around. Only silence.

An overlay of the city kept flickering into view. It was disorienting to see both worlds at the same time. *Is it always like this for the professor,* she wondered. *Or is this what happens when The Great Invention is unbalanced?* Cars sat lined up at traffic lights, the sky glowed vibrantly, and trees with huge bell-shaped flowers hung over the store fronts.

Tessa tried to move toward the street but kept walking into thorny brambles. It was hard to see either world clearly. "Where do I go!" Tessa yelled in frustration. Forcing herself to ignore the shimmery flickers of the street, Tessa turned slowly in a circle, looking for a way through the brambly woods.

Then, rising out of a tangle of vines, Tessa spotted a thin black ribbon-like road that twisted steeply up until it was above the trees. It looked to Tessa like a

Hot Wheels track, flimsy and almost too narrow to walk on, but it seemed to be her only option.

Carefully she made her way over to it. It was about two feet wide and sloped upward until it plateaued 20 feet above the ground. *Well, at least I'm not scared of heights*, she said to herself.

As she stepped onto the black track, the whole thing moved under her. It reminded her of the little bouncy bridges that connect jungle gyms, but this one didn't have a railing.

With one foot in front of the other, her arms extended like a tightrope walker, Tessa walked up the steep path, trying to keep the road as steady as possible. It was an odd sensation to be walking up to treetop level without railings. She might have loved it in another context, but at this moment, the slow careful steps made her feel like she'd never get to the end, and she willed herself to be patient. "Hodges!" she called every few minutes, peering over the edge and straining her ears for an answer. *Could he be somewhere with the professor?*

Tessa saw a great rock wall in the distance and immediately recognized it from her dream. A shiver shot through her as she remembered Gus lying at the bottom. "Hodges!" she yelled more urgently. She could tell now that the road was sloping toward the top of the cliff. She hurried, walking as fast as she dared as the road lurched beneath her.

Suddenly, a flock of black birds, each the size of Tessa's forearm, dove out of the sky and flew in front of her, squawking and screaming. Tessa shrieked, almost losing her balance. The mob of birds whizzed past her, and then, as if they were one creature, turned around and headed back toward her.

"Get out of here!" she yelled, waving her arms as they approached. The road bounced. The birds flew so close to her face that Tessa could see the sharpness of their beaks. She ducked and huddled on her hands and knees waiting for them to pass. But the mass of birds banked and came at her again. She scrunched into a ball as they blew past her, cackling!

Carefully, Tessa crawled a few steps forward until, again, the birds swooped toward her. *How will I make it?* she thought, looking ahead at the cliffs. She scrunched down and braced herself just in time as the birds ripped through the air above her. Tessa squeezed her eyes shut and this time claws scraped across her back.

"Ahhhhhhhhhh!" Tessa could hardly hear her own scream in the swarm of cawing birds. Were they trying to knock her off? The scratches on her back stung.

"Help!" she cried, her nose inches from the road. "Help!"

The birds receded again, and from somewhere far away, Tessa heard someone yell, "No!" Her head shot up. She couldn't see anyone, but for a second, the flock of birds seemed almost to fly in place, as if it were caught in an invisible net. Tessa's heart beat faster.

"No!" This scream was louder, and the birds, though flapping just as hard, started slowly moving backwards as if a huge wind pushed them.

Tessa sat up and stared. Even though the air was still, the birds were actually blowing away. Slowly, she stood up, entranced, as she watched the vicious birds get smaller and smaller until she couldn't see them anymore.

Tessa's whole body relaxed. The birds were gone. "Hello?" she called eagerly to the unmoving woods. No answer. "Hellooooooo!" Someone out there had helped her. Though her legs were shaky, Tessa started to walk, scanning below for the person who'd screamed.

"Tessa!" The voice was far away, but she recognized it immediately.

"I'm here! I'm here!" she yelled, waving her arms. "Hodges!" She looked wildly around trying to spot him. There up ahead at the top of the cliff, she saw Hodges waving and calling. Tessa tried her best not to jump up and down and jostle herself off the flimsy road. Carefully she and Hodges hurried toward each other. "How'd you know I was here?" Tessa called.

"Allergia," Hodges said. "The birds."

"Allergia?" Tessa felt alarm ring through her body, and she instinctively looked around. "Sent the birds! Where's she now?"

He pulled a river rock from his pocket.

"Did you *hit* her?"

Hodges nodded.

"Wow!" Tessa wondered if she would have been that bold. "Impressive. You've always had the best aim!" Hodges was close enough to grab now, and Tessa pulled him into a hug. "Thanks," she said into his hair. "I'm so happy to see you."

Together they wobbled off the bouncy road to the top of the cliff.

"Gus —" Hodges started to say, and his face looked sad.

"I know," Tessa interrupted. "I saw your dad. Michael brought Gus home." Hodges nodded. "And he's with your mom at the hospital. He's ok," she said with more certainty than she felt. "He's going to be ok," she said again to convince herself. "I'm so glad I found you! Or, really you found me." Tessa smiled. "Have you been here since Gus fell?"

Hodges nodded and pointed to a large flat rock where he'd apparently been sitting. It was dusted with crumbs. "The professor."

"I can tell. Was it cookies?" said Tessa smiling. Hodges nodded. Suddenly Tessa remembered why they'd separated and felt a shock of awkwardness. Did Hodges know she'd talked to Bronken? She looked down at her shoes. "I'm — I'm really sorry I left. I shouldn't have done that."

Hodges took her hand and squeezed it.

Tessa took a deep breath.

Suddenly, the compass vibrated, and they both jolted. It read: **UNTIL THE END OF THE ERA: 1 Day, 9 Hours, 23 minutes**.

"One day?? But what about Gus!" Tessa said, sagging at the thought of looking for The Great Invention without him. "We *have* to get to The Great Invention. But I think we need to see Gus first."

Hodges nodded and started walking.

"How can we get to him from here?" Tessa said,

looking around blankly.

Hodges pointed to a polished wooden door standing at the edge of the forest floor. It was dark and worn and covered with vines. Tessa hadn't even noticed it.

"What in the world —" Tessa began.

"Professor left it," said Hodges, reaching for the knob.

CHAPTER 32

The door opened into the warm sitting room of the professor's house. Today the cushions were bright yellow, and the curtains had big oranges and bananas printed all over them. The room felt sunny, despite the stormy weather outside.

"Hello?" Tessa called. "Anyone home?"

Hodges stepped up to the table, and Tessa noticed two blueberry muffins sitting on a plate with a small note beside them:

T and H-

Time is short. Find G. What you need starts there.

-Prof. H

Tessa read the words aloud twice. "Why couldn't he just say 'you need blah blah blah, and it's under Gus's bed or something?'" She sighed. "At least he knows where we are." She picked up a muffin and broke off the roof. It was perfectly crispy around the edges, and the cake-part was crammed with berries. "Mmmmm. His food is the best!" Hodges had blueberry smudges around his mouth already. "Let's go," Tessa said, popping the rest of her muffin in her mouth.

$$* * *$$

As soon as Hodges opened the front door of his house, Tessa felt nervous. "Hello?" she called tentatively.

"Hey," Gus's tired voice came from the other room and sounded scratchy.

"You're home!" Relief flooded her, and she rushed into the room. He lay stretched out on the living room couch. The whole right side of his face was skinned, and he had a fat lip. His right hand was bandaged, and patches of gauze were taped in various places on his legs and arms.

Hodges put his head on Gus's chest in a gentle kind of hug, and Gus wrapped his good arm around his brother. "You're ok," Gus said, and Tessa could tell he'd been worried. Hodges nodded his agreement.

"You look pretty bad," Tessa said, trying to smile as tears burned her eyes. She blinked quickly and sat down on the coffee table next to him. "This is my fault," she said quietly.

"Your fault?" he asked surprised.

"I should never have left." Tessa avoided Gus's eyes, studying the weave of the couch pillow instead. "And I shouldn't have talked to Bronken."

"You talked to Bronken?"

The disbelief on Gus's face almost made Tessa lose her courage. She shifted uncomfortably but went on. "He pretended to be such a nice guy. He... I don't know, he said we needed help, and it made sense—" She paused. "I believed him."

Gus didn't say anything for a minute. "When I was climbing, Bronken said you were helping him," Gus said. "But I thought he was lying."

She swallowed hard. "I wasn't *helping* him. But I did talk to him." Her eyes bore into the rug as she rushed on. "And I think that's how he knew to come after you rock climbing." Her eyes darted to Gus's face. "I'm so sorry. I had no idea he could do this..." Tessa felt sick as she looked again at Gus's banged up body. "Then last night I had this dream that you were rock climbing, and Hodges was high on the wall, and Bronken came. He was telling you all this stuff about Hodges falling, until you froze and couldn't climb anymore. Then I saw him make a huge rock hit your hand, and you lost your grip and fell."

Gus's eyes were wide. "That's exactly what happened."

Tessa nodded. "I watched it. But I thought it was just a dream. When I woke up, I came over to make sure you were OK, and your dad told me you were at the ER. I couldn't believe it. I still can't." Tessa's eyes darted between the nubby blue wool of the rug and Gus's face. "I'm so sorry."

"I can't believe you dreamed that," said Gus.

"Me neither," Tessa said shaking her head. "But it got me over here. And then your dad gave me this to help me find a door." She held up the new vider.

"My dad had a *vider*?" He turned to Hodges who shrugged and for the first time didn't seem to know exactly what was going on.

Tessa nodded. "He knew everything before I even told him. He said they've known from the beginning that we had the Ultimate."

"How——?"

"I don't know. But this one is just a regular vider, not the Ultimate one. Apparently there are different kinds. And your parents used to see the Unseen with it, but they can't anymore. I don't know why. He said they'll explain later."

"Why didn't they *tell* us!" Gus asked in disbelief.

"Books and songs," Hodges said.

Gus looked at his brother. "Making books and singing songs? That doesn't count as telling us anything!" he protested.

"Are they home?" Tessa asked hopefully.

"No," said Gus. "They're at the pharmacy picking up some cream for my face and then had to stop by my dad's office, but I think they'll be home soon."

"Your dad said they'd always wanted us to find out about the Unseen. After we went to the professor's house," Tessa continued, "they were planning to talk to us, but then they saw we had the Ultimate Vider, and they knew they didn't have time. Your dad said they had no idea how deep in we were. I guess I didn't either ..." She looked at the gash above Gus's eye.

Gus interrupted her thought. "But if they knew all of that, why weren't they helping us? I mean, why didn't they help me on the cliff or rescue Hodges?"

"I asked that, too." Tessa said. "Your dad said they can't get into the Unseen anymore. I don't know why."

Gus threw up his good hand, exasperated and excited at once. Tessa saw Gus's sketchbook on the coffee table opened to a blank page with a few pencils and a coin beside it.

"Hodges, is that the coin you found?" Tessa asked.

"Yep," Hodges said. "Gave it to Gus." Gus picked it up absentmindedly, rubbing his thumb along the edge while he thought. No one talked for a minute, and the ticking compass sounded loud in the quiet living room.

"How much time's left?" Gus asked.

Hodges held the compass so they could all see the words:

UNTIL THE END OF THE ERA: 1 Day, 8 Hours, 12 Minutes.

CHAPTER 33

"A day and a half...." Tessa looked at Gus lying there.

"I think I'm fine," Gus said, slowly sitting up and swinging his legs onto the floor.

"Really?" Tessa asked doubtfully.

Gus flinched as he pushed himself to standing. "Yeah, it's just my knee," he said wincing. "I landed on a rock and have a bunch of stitches by the side of my kneecap. They said I can try to walk though. I'll just be sore." He hobbled slowly across the living room then leaned against the wall. The little color in his cheeks drained from his face.

"I'm not sure you can make it," Tessa said apologetically.

He looked over at the door still ten feet away and

leaned against the wall. Tessa watched him absent-mindedly flip the coin and catch it over and over as he considered what to do. "You're getting pretty good at that," she offered, nodding toward the coin.

"Oh, I didn't even notice I was doing it," Gus said. The coin glinted in the light as he flipped it through the air again.

"Time." Hodges was looking out the window.

"Time to go?" Tessa asked. She looked anxiously at Gus. "I don't want to go without you." Hodges was nodding. "But, we may have to?"

"I can at least try to spot a door from the porch," said Gus, already starting to hobble toward the door again. "We've found a door every time we've needed one so far," he said confidently.

"Eventually," Tessa muttered under her breath.

The three kids stood on the front porch scanning the street. They used both viders, and Tessa could tell Gus felt especially determined to spot something. As he slowly surveyed the scene, he rubbed his thumb along the ridge of the coin he held. "It's funny," he said, interrupting the silence. "If I were blindfolded, I'd be sure this thing was one of my camera lenses. It feels just like it." He weighed the coin on his palm.

"Could," Hodges said.

"Could what?"

"Work."

"On my camera?" Gus held the coin up and looked closely at it.

"No, vider."

Gus shot Hodges a skeptical look. "As a lens? But it's opaque!" Even as Gus said it, he was trying to twist the coin onto the wide end of the vider. It screwed perfectly into place.

"That looks more like a lens *cap*," said Tessa frowning.

"Totally," Gus agreed. But he tried it out anyway, and his jaw dropped. "This *is* a lens!"

"What? What do you see?" Tessa leaned over as if she could share the view.

He was pointing the vider all over the place. "Look!" He thrust the capped vider at Tessa.

He was right. Tessa could see sunlight suddenly in the dense cloudy sky, and for the first time, the whole neighborhood glowed. She hadn't noticed before, but now she saw Michael standing down the block and other people in glowy clothes walking on paths that wound through the air among the houses. Brilliant white creatures were everywhere! Wide-winged birds in the sky, pixie-like animals with long wispy tufts of hair, and over where the trees were denser, huge creatures whose shapes Tessa couldn't quite make out.

"What *is* this?" she asked.

"I don't know! And we've never seen the animals before!" Gus glanced at Hodges who sat giggling and squirming, pushing the air in front of him away. Tessa looked at Hodges through the vider: Two animals, like small shaggy white kangaroos with tufts of tall cottony hair standing straight up on their heads burrowed into Hodges's lap.

"Packasindrias!" Hodges shrieked.

Their long hair, that inexplicably stood straight up from their heads at least a foot high, tickled Hodges's chin as the two creatures butted against his chest. Slowly, Tessa reached her hand toward one and was surprised the animal didn't flinch when she got close.

"Oh my gosh!" she yelled. "It's SO soft! Like a chinchilla!" She studied its scruffy white face and big black eyes through the vider, then buried her nose in the soft fountain of hair on its head, laughing.

Gus watched her grope the air in front of Hodges. "What are you guys doing?"

Reluctantly Tessa released the Packasindria she was hugging and handed Gus the vider. It did look funny to see him reach out and pet the air. Tessa tried to pet it again, too, reaching around blindly, and instantly her fingers sank into soft fur she couldn't see. "I can still feel it!" she shrieked. "Even though I can't see it!"

"We've never been able to do this before!" Gus said, looking between Tessa and the vider.

"Do you think," Tessa paused considering her own question, "it's because this lens is much stronger or because the barrier between the Seen and the Unseen is getting weaker?"

"Oh," said Gus, his face growing serious. He turned and scanned the street again as if he'd just remembered their mission.

But Tessa couldn't stop touching the Packasindria's head.

"Wait," Gus said, shaking the vider. "There's something wrong with this. Everything's flickering."

The paths that had been so bright at first were fading here and there. Even Michael was flickering.

"These can't break, right?" Gus asked.

"Time," said Hodges again.

"Running out of time?" Tessa asked.

"Running out of time makes the vider weaker?" Gus clarified, "because The Great Invention isn't working very well?"

Hodges nodded.

194

Tessa shuttered, remembering what the professor had said. If the Invention stopped, love would stop. And Wholehearteds. Tessa tried to imagine a world run by Shellstalkers. "It can't already be broken!"

"Need the other." Hodges said.

"Other what?" Gus asked.

"Lens," said Hodges brightly.

"*What* other lens?" Gus asked.

"Adam's."

His word hung in the air for an instant before Tessa yelled, "Ohmigosh!!! My *dad* has a lens!" She jumped to her feet. "On his keys! We have to get to my house! He leaves his keys in a dish on the counter! Be right back, Gus!" Tessa was already careening down the front steps. She barged through the front door and ran into the kitchen with Hodges at her heels.

"Hello, oh loud one!" Cassie hollered from upstairs.

"Hi Cass!" Tessa yelled. The green ceramic dish on the counter was empty.

"Oh no!" Tessa moaned to Hodges. "He must have taken them with him to New York! Cassie!" she called up the stairs, "when's Dad back?"

"After dinner," Cassie called. "You ok? Feels like I haven't seen you in days!"

"I know! Yeah, I'm good!"

Tessa heard thudding footsteps above her, and Cassie appeared at the top of the stairs with tissues wedged between her toes. She was walking on her heels. "Brooke's painting my nails," she explained as Brooke's face popped over the banister. She waved to Tessa. "Molly comes Friday!" Cassie called. "In just four days!"

Tessa's heart surged. "Let's see if Loochie will make maduros for her!"

"She will! She knows they're Molly's favorite!"

"How about youuuu ask Loochie," Tessa teased. "At least you can drive away and escape if she starts complaining."

Cassie laughed. "But what if Loochie wants to stay for dinner, too?"

"Oh pretty please, no!" Tessa said.

Hodges held up the compass. It glowed again.

"I've gotta go — love you! And bye Brooke!"

"Bye!" both girls called together.

"Hodges," Tessa said as they left the house. "I think we need your parents."

CHAPTER 34

"His keys are in New York!" Tessa moaned to Gus, as Mika and Marcus pulled up and creaked into park.

"Hodges!" Mika yelled, launching herself from the passenger's seat and swallowing him in a hug. "You're safe!"

Marcus wrapped his arms around both of them. "So happy to see you, little man." He kissed the top of Hodges's head. "And you're outside!" he said, looking up at Gus. "How are you feeling?"

"Ok," Gus said, shifting his weight to his good leg. "My knee just hurts. But Dad — why didn't you tell us you had a vider!"

Marcus shook his head. "Oh man. I wish we'd told you everything right away! We had no idea how fast things were moving."

"Or that you were in any danger," Mika cut in quickly. Her eyes were sad as she touched Gus's cheek. "I'm sorry we didn't pay more attention. We just assumed — we should have asked more questions." Then she turned to Tessa. "Tess, all of this was your mom! She lived for the Unseen."

"My mom?" Tessa's heart skipped a beat. She'd been wondering ever since they'd talked to Michael. "Was she —" all of a sudden Tessa felt embarrassed to ask the question that had been burning in her. She forced herself to say the words. "Was she like Hodges?"

Mika's eyes brightened. "Yes! Your mom was Wholehearted!"

Tessa nodded, her eyes suddenly brimming with tears. Her mom had been a Wholehearted? Tessa wished more than ever her mom were here. She had so many questions now.

Mika pulled Tessa close. "I miss her too, Tessa girl. She would have loved to teach you about this." Tessa leaned into Mika's arms.

"We only have a day and 8 hours left," Gus cut in, bringing them back to the moment. "But we can't do anything without Tessa's dad."

Marcus raised his eyebrows.

"He has a lens," Gus explained.

"A lens! Oh! Remember the lenses?" Marcus asked Mika excitedly.

"Cassie said he'll be home after dinner," Tessa continued, pulling out her phone. "Oh! He just texted!" She scrolled through his message. "No!" she groaned. "He has to stay in New York for dinner and isn't coming home till tomorrow now! We're going to run out of time!"

"No, you're not," said Mika. Her tone carried such certainty that no one argued. "Come on, everyone," she said, and put her arm around Gus's shoulder to help him walk into the house.

✳ ✳ ✳

"This waiting gives us a chance to talk," said Mika, pulling out the stools around the kitchen counter. The kids sat down, and Marcus dumped chips in a bowl and filled water glasses.

"We want to know everything," Gus said. "How'd you get a vider? And meet the professor? And, seriously, why didn't you ever tell us!"

"All good questions," said Marcus.

"We'll start at the beginning," Mika said. "Before

you guys were born, the four of us — your parents, Tessa, and the two of us — flew to California to travel through the state parks."

"Right," said Tessa. She'd looked through her parents' photo albums from that trip dozens of times and had studied the pictures. Their parents had just finished college and had soft round faces. Her dad's shaggy hair touched his shoulders, and her mom wore platform sandals. Mika was in a silver jewelry phase and had rings on every finger. Marcus had been bald even then.

Gus pulled out his sketchbook and a pencil as he listened. It reminded Tessa of English class. Gus always said he listened better when he was drawing. He was already sketching the vider with the lens on the end and a dozen sharp arrows pointing to it. LENS, he wrote in jagged letters so the S looked like a backwards Z.

"We flew into Sacramento," Mika continued, "and drove straight to the coast. Remember those morning glory muffins in Mendocino? I'm still trying to recreate those. Anyway, we took three weeks to drive down the coast. We had this tiny rental car and kept rotating who had to cram into the backseat — remember that?" Mika said.

"I think my knees still remember that," Marcus said laughing.

"We loved everywhere we went, but your mom couldn't get over Big Sur! A narrow road winds along these towering cliffs — it's very dramatic. Your mom insisted on driving that whole stretch and kept pulling us over to take pictures. Some guy told us we could find jade down in a cove at low tide, so your mom made us walk through a field of poison oak to the beach to hunt for some."

"She found a real piece of jade, too! I think she was the only one whose heart was in the hunt," said Marcus.

"What's this trip have to do with the vider?" Gus asked, trying to hurry them up.

"Wait," Tessa interrupted, picturing her mom's face beaming in an orange kayak. "Where was that aquarium where you kayaked with otters?" That picture was one of Tessa's favorites. She'd framed it and put it by her bed.

"Oh, that was in Monterey, a bit north. That's an incredible aquarium! We'll have to go there one day," said Marcus. "Wow, we could give you a play-by-play of this trip all night!"

"Right," said Mika. "Let's fast forward."

"We finally ended up south of L.A. Our last stop was Catalina Island." Marcus leaned toward the California map Gus had just finished outlining and pointed to the very bottom of it. "The island is just about there, off the coast. You have to take a ferry to get there. Our plan was to camp for one night."

"With the bison!" said Mika.

"Bison are on an island?" Gus asked.

"Yeah, apparently, some L.A. film producer brought them out there in the 1920s for a movie shoot and left them! I think Mika has a whole sketchbook of bison from that trip!" Marcus laughed.

Mika smiled affectionatlely at him and turned back to the kids. "And Catalina," she continued, "is where the story really begins."

CHAPTER 35

"Why?" asked Gus. "What happened on Catalina?" He jiggled his good leg impatiently.

"Rowah," Marcus said. "While we were camping, we met a woman named Rowah. She was—"

"She was free," Mika finished.

"She was," Marcus agreed, and it seemed to Tessa he emphasized the word "was," but he kept talking before she could ask. "That night we made a huge campfire, and Rowah, who was camping, too, joined us. She brought a drum and sang all night, until none of us could keep our eyes open! She had the most beautiful voice. We'd never heard music like hers."

"We were only supposed to stay on Catalina one night, but we didn't want to leave her. She was magnetic! We ended up staying for *five* nights, just to be with her longer. We snorkeled all day and climbed around tide pools with her while she talked to us about seeing. Remember those tidepools, Marcus? I'd never touched sea anemones before or those giant sea stars — and sea hares!"

"What's a sea hare?" Gus asked scrunching up his nose.

"The softest thing in the world! You must hold one someday!" Mika's eyes were dancing as she looked at Tessa, and Tessa couldn't help but smile. "Your mom kept picking them up — they're like these giant sea slugs, but not slimy, just melt-in-your-hands soft. I don't know if you're supposed to pick them up, but she held every one that we found. She was obsessed."

Tessa knew right away what Mika was talking about. There was a picture of her mom, her head thrown back laughing, holding a brown blob the length of a shoe box. Tessa definitely wanted to hold one of those someday. Her chest ached as she imagined her mom handing the slippery creature to her, laughing as hard as she had in the photo. Maybe one day Tessa could go to California with Molly and retrace their steps. The thought perked her up, but didn't take the ache away.

"Anyway," Marcus took over. "Rowah talked about

how the most important thing in life was to see through the visible to what's inside, to see the Unseen. It was radically different than anything we'd ever heard. We'd just finished college, and everyone was telling us that the most important things were to land a solid job, to make a lot of money, to save for a house —— but Rowah kept talking about seeing the Unseen and about paying attention."

"And when she looked at us, she really *was* paying attention," Mika said. "She *saw* us. Rowah was different than anyone I'd ever met before."

"Different than anyone any of us had ever known," Marcus agreed.

"I remember thinking I wanted to be just like her." Mika smiled, but Tessa noticed her eyes looked sad. "We all did back then. Before it got complicated."

"That week everything was simple," said Marcus, picking the story up. "We drank in everything she said and everything she sang."

"Do you remember any of her songs?" Gus asked.

"Of course," said Mika. "They became a part of us." She started humming, closed her eyes and swayed with the melody. Tessa recognized the tune right away.

"That song?" said Gus.

"Familiar, isn't it?" said Mika, smiling as she opened

her eyes.

"You hum that *all* the time."

"My mom used to sing it also!" Tessa said, surprised. "But I didn't know it was anything special."

"Songs always are," Mika said. "I think you'd recognize most of the songs we learned there. Songs are funny that way — they can become a part of you, and you don't even notice. Songs are powerful — they connect us, and even protect us."

"Protect us how?" Gus asked.

"It's hard to explain, but they connect us to the fabric of the Unseen, where singing always happens."

"That's how we first learned about Gloria," Marcus added. "Through the songs."

"And we fell in love with her, too!" Mika said. "During the trip, Rowah told us all about herself — or at least we thought she did." Mika gave Marcus a dark look. "And it turned out she lived on the east coast, too, right here in Washington, D.C.! Go figure. We'd traveled to California to meet our neighbor!"

"What do you mean, you thought she'd told you about herself?" Tessa asked, curious about the way Mika had looked at Marcus.

"Well, it got complicated later," Mika said. "But that summer, after our trip, we started going to her house every week. She hosted a dinner every Tuesday night, and anyone could come. We met the professor for the first time there and learned about Wholehearteds. We'd spend the evenings eating stew and homemade bread, listening to stories and singing. We started to see the world differently after being with that group," Mika said.

"Sounds like a hippie love-fest, Mom," Gus said.

Mika laughed. "But so much better! Rowah didn't seem to care about anything we cared about, not clothes, or where people lived, or what they looked like, not power or government — and you know that's rare in D.C.!"

"No one there did. They just cared about seeing each other and living deeply," Marcus said.

"They really were free."

"So where did this vider and Adam's lens come from?" Gus asked, seeming impatient for the story to catch up to them.

"Those came from the professor," said Marcus. "He gave us that vider to use for a little while —"

"But you still have it!" Gus cut in.

"Oh, I should say he gave it to us to keep, but only to use for a little while," Marcus clarified.

"What do you mean?" Tessa asked.

"We can't see the Unseen world like you're seeing it anymore," said Marcus. "That's just the way it is. Wholehearteds always get to, but the rest of us, if we're lucky, are given a glimpse just long enough to teach us. So for a little while, while we were learning, we could see through the vider like you are. We saw those vibrant colors! And the complexity of people. We saw battles happening, and Shellstalkers in the clouds."

"The Shellstalkers are in the clouds?" Tessa thought of the low stormy skies they'd had all week. "That's seriously creepy." She couldn't help but shiver.

"Then our vider stopped working. Our job became remembering the Unseen and listening for the deeper parts of people that we can't see with our eyes. The Unseen takes faith now," said Marcus. "One day you'll have to lean on faith, too."

"And sing," said Hodges.

Mika smiled. "Yes, always sing. Our singing, even in the kitchen, strengthens the Wholehearteds and makes the Unseen sharper and more beautiful. It helps the battles."

"So that's why I couldn't help you find Hodges, Tessa," Marcus said. "We can't move into the Unseen world anymore. I just know it's there, and when I sing,

I can sense it."

Gus had stopped drawing and was studying his mom and dad.

"What battles are you talking about?" asked Gus.

"The professor," said Hodges.

"That's right," Marcus said. "Wholehearteds are constantly in battles resisting the Shellstalkers and maintaining the balance."

Hodges yawned.

"It's getting late," Marcus said, "but to finish answering your question about the vider: the professor gave us ours one Valentine's Day."

"I was hoping for chocolate, personally," Mika laughed.

"But instead, he brought a puzzle. It looked like a metal box, almost like a Rubik's Cube. There were panels around the sides that slid and turned. Buttons, too?" Mika nodded. "We had to get the combination right for the whole thing to open. We all tried, but none of us could figure it out. Mika's especially good at puzzles ——"

"Yeah, Gus got that from you," Tessa interjected.

"Yeah," Marcus agreed. "And after working on it for two solid days, Mika eventually opened it. Inside was something else metal that we had to take apart, the next part of the puzzle. When we finally finished and disassembled the whole thing, we had the box, a compass, a lens, and a vider."

"They all connected?" said Gus.

"Yes," said Mika noticing Hodges slumped in the kitchen chair, asleep now. She brushed his hair from his eyes and looked up at the clock. "It's almost 11, you guys! No wonder! I have a feeling tomorrow's going to be a huge day. We all need to sleep."

"We can't!" Tessa protested.

"Just think of it as an intermission," said Mika smiling. "Tessa, want to sleep here since your dad's still gone?"

"Sure," she said. "I'll go tell Cassie and grab my stuff."

"I'll make up the futon in my studio for you."

CHAPTER 36

Tessa woke up early full of energy. She threw on her clothes, sent her dad a quick good-morning text, and crammed her pajamas into the backpack she'd brought over. She could hear dishes clinking in the kitchen and smell bacon.

"Good morning!" said Marcus as Tessa opened the door. Gus's hair was mashed on the side and sticking up, and Hodges's eyes looked sleepy, but both boys were already holding plates of fried eggs.

"Morning," smiled Tessa. Her phone vibrated, and she pulled it out to see a text from her dad. "My dad gets in at 3:00 today," she read. "And needs a ride! I guess Cassie's getting her oil changed and can't go. Could we pick him up?" she asked eagerly.

"No problem," said Marcus.

"Can't he come earlier?" Gus asked.

"Guess not," said Tessa picking up a hot piece of bacon with her fingers. "He always takes the earliest train he can, and I told him we need him as soon as possible." She picked up the Ultimate Vider from the table where Gus had left it and looked at her bacon with it. It didn't change. "I guess bacon doesn't have feelings," she said laughing. "You have the other vider, right Gus?"

"Yeah, I've been experimenting. It doesn't seem to do too much," he said, shoving his sketch book across the counter toward Tessa. He'd drawn the new vider and what looked like a projection coming out of it, showing the kitchen. Question marks surrounded it, and he'd printed STAYS THE SAME? in big letters.

"It's mostly for doors," said Marcus.

"Maybe it'll help later," said Tessa shrugging. "Let's bring it. But don't mix them up! Not that we really could, but I'll carry this one for now," said Tessa, pushing the Ultimate Vider into her jean shorts pocket. "And you keep that one."

Mika was the last to the kitchen and wore a pale pink fluffy bathrobe. Marcus poured her a mug of hot water as she dug through the jar of teabags. "Thanks," she said to him. "How are you feeling this morning?"

she asked Gus.

"A lot better." He hopped off his chair and walked across the room. "I fell asleep with the ice pack on and took medicine when I woke up, like the doctor said. Seems like it worked!" His face looked better, too, Tessa noticed. It was still scraped up, but his lip wasn't swollen anymore.

A sharp buzzing vibrated the room, and they all ducked instinctively. Hodges pointed toward the kitchen sink, and Tessa looked just in time to see the professor's pencils pop out of nowhere and swipe a black window in the air.

Singing poured into the Tuckers' kitchen, a mass of voices tied together like rope. The sound made Tessa feel strong, and at the same time sent goosebumps flying up her arms. She glanced at Gus, who looked ready to spring into action.

"A battle song," Mika breathed from behind them.

Battle, yes, Tessa thought, *that's just what it feels like.* "Professor?" Tessa called toward the window. She knew he must be close, though the opening remained pitch black.

"He's singing," said Hodges matter-of-factly as he pulled himself onto the counter. Before anyone could respond, Hodges jumped into the darkness and was gone.

"Oh!" Mika yelped.

"Hodges!" Gus clamored up on the counter after him and nervously poked his head into the dark hole. "I can't see anything in here!"

Tessa climbed up beside him. "The music's louder!" Her heart started beating faster, though she didn't know why. She looked over to Mika for help, and Mika gave a sharp nod. "C'mon," Tessa said, and without giving Gus time to reply, she grabbed his arm and jumped after Hodges.

CHAPTER 37

They tumbled onto the ground behind Hodges. Tessa looked nervously at Gus, worried he'd fallen on his knee, but he seemed fine and was already standing up in the giant woodsy field where they'd landed. Hundreds of people stood around them, all wearing glistening white clothes and singing. Professor Henchworth wildly conducted them as they walked through the grass. Though the professor sang with an unexpectedly rich voice, and though the song itself sounded serious, Tessa and Gus couldn't help laughing. They weren't laughing *at* the professor. It was more like they felt a surging happiness as they listened to the music. Others seemed to feel the same as trills of laughter wove through the melody. Tessa breathed in the cool grassy air and for a brief second, closed her eyes. Between the air and the   music, she felt like she was flying.

They fell into step with the crowd, and as they walked, the kids found themselves humming. It was impossible not to join in, even though they didn't know the song.

"Where do you think we're going?" Gus asked. The group was definitely walking with purpose. "We can't exactly ask the professor!" He laughed as they watched the professor sing and hop and dance as if he were making music with his entire body.

The breeze blew Tessa's dark curls around her face, and she brimmed with happiness as they walked.

Gus glanced around. "What do you think my parents meant when they said this song is a *battle* — not a real battle, right?"

Tessa couldn't imagine what they'd meant in this world of color and song.

"Shellstalkers." The second Hodges said it, the music jerked like a DJ had scratched the record, and then it returned to normal.

Tessa could only see the field of singing people and the green crowns of trees. She looked down at Hodges. *Were Shellstalkers here too?* Again, the music snagged and became discordant. Tessa checked to see the professor's reaction, but he looked unphased and sang more heartily than ever.

Suddenly a noise crashed so loudly that Tessa couldn't pick out the professor's melody from the clatter of cymbals, screeches, and half chords that had exploded around her. A loud muffled voice suddenly cut in. Tessa strained to hear what it said.

TESSATHIS WAY FJRM COME THIS WY-WAYYY

"Someone said my name!" Tessa called. The voice felt strangely compelling.

"Come on, we have to stay with the professor!" Gus urged.

"Yeah, I know..." Tessa said, her voice dropping off. Even as she urged herself to keep pace, Tessa slowed down to listen.

RRACOME NWWDARM HELP NEED SLKJ YOUDFO TESSA!

She stopped, straining to hear what the voice was saying. Who was calling her? What were they trying to tell her?

Gus's mouth was moving, but Tessa couldn't hear him in all the noise. "I can't understand you!" she yelled. "I think the voice is coming from back there!" Already Tessa was turning around and pushing past people. The racket grew, and everyone was moving in different directions. Tessa hurried back the way they'd come, trying to catch another snippet. She couldn't hear the singing at all anymore and didn't even notice the people she passed. Every cell in her body drew her toward the voice. Gus was hurrying beside her, yelling something, but she couldn't hear him.

TESSA RAISENT COME THE WE MEWEN WILL HELP YOUUS EOIDOAT GUS

Tessa still could only decipher a few words, but the pull was magnetic, and she began to jog. The noise around her was deafening now, and the crowd felt endless. She pushed on, feeling almost dizzy as she fought to concentrate on the voice. She no longer had a sense of where she was or where she was going, just that she had to continue.

Suddenly out of nowhere, Hodges lunged for her arm. His hand felt hot on her skin, and Tessa shook him off, annoyed. He pulled on her again.

"Get off me!" she yelled. His eyes looked hurt and urgent as she shook free, breaking into a full run. She'd never talked to Hodges like that before, but he clearly didn't understand what she was doing.

The calling grew louder, and Tessa knew she was close now. A group of people hurried toward her, looking expectant. They smiled and ushered her on. The deep smooth voice felt like a current. TESSA, it boomed. She kept coming.

Her head felt full of cotton as the people reached out welcoming her. They put their arms around her. *Were they talking?* Tessa searched their friendly faces. In the clash of broken music, only the voice remained a steady note, and she gravitated to it. She couldn't think straight. Every thought swam away before it even formed, but these people were helping her.

Then the voice was loud! Tessa had walked close enough to decipher the words clearly: THE VIDER—

Yes, the vider! I have the vider. She patted her pocket.

The faces around her smiled and nodded their encouragement, standing in a tight crowd around her. They were walking fast now, and all she could hear in the loud windy noise was the singular voice that now boomed inside of her.

YOU'VE MADE IT!

The group was celebrating, laughing around her. Tessa smiled a confused smile and nodded.

A BURDEN. THE VIDER WAS A BURDEN—

Tessa's pocket suddenly felt heavy. The vider weighed against her leg so heavily that she found it difficult to walk. The vider *was* a burden.

YOU'RE SO TIRED.

Tessa's head pounded. Everything was so loud. Her arms and legs felt like they weighed 100 pounds each. She was exhausted! The people around her gave her sympathetic looks as they crowded close and moved her on.

YOU'VE DONE GREAT— YOU CAN LET IT GO NOW.

The voice echoed through Tessa's body. She reached into her jean shorts and felt the vider, so heavy now in her hand.

LET IT GO. YOU CAN LET IT ALL GO, AND BE FREE.

Free. The word made her feel like she was leaving the ground, light as a breeze. *Free!* She pulled out the vider, and the air vibrated with a cool misty feeling. The vider felt like lead. It would feel so good to be free.

YES, THERE YOU GO, TESSA. GREAT WORK!

She was doing great work! She felt her face blush with pride as she looked at the people surrounding her. Tessa moved her arm slowly like it was underwater.

The handsome man with intensely dark eyes who stood in front of her seemed to be speaking. He looked familiar, and he was so proud of her. Everyone smiled.

THANK YOU, said the man, reaching out his hand. Tessa placed the vider in his palm, and as she did, a cold gust of air blasted her face so hard it took her breath away.

Instantly her head cleared, and the professor's brilliant music burst back into her ears.

Bronken's face was inches from her own, and though her fingers were still around the vider, he was holding it, too.

CHAPTER 38

"Don't!" Gus yelled. He grabbed Tessa's arm, but it was too late.

"I can't move!" Tessa screamed, trying to pull her hand away from Bronken's.

The professor appeared next to her with the sea of Wholehearteds close behind. Tessa could sense them swaying and moving as they sang.

Tessa jerked the vider as hard as she could, but it wouldn't budge. Somehow it was connected to Bronken and so was she!

"Why can't I move?!" she yelled. Bronken's face looked angry now, and rage burned in the eyes of the crowd behind him.

"Let go." She heard his deep voice reverberate in her head.

"Don't let go!" Gus urged. "Don't let them have it! They tricked you to get us over here. Hold on to it!"

Drums began to sound. Tessa couldn't see the instruments, but a fast soulful beating rose around her. More Wholehearteds! She tightened her grip. "No," she said bravely.

The Wholehearteds' singing pressed like a warm wind against her back, supporting her.

The vider started to feel cold. Tessa felt the professor looking at her, and she looked away as her cheeks burned with embarrassment. *I'm such an idiot! How could I possibly have walked up to Bronken and given him the vider!* She glanced at the professor, braced for his anger.

Instead, the twinkling-eyed, crooked-toothed professor sang.

"I'm so sorry," she whispered.

He smiled at her through every wrinkle and belted out a melody so loud and boisterous that Tessa couldn't help but almost laugh. She tried again to pull the vider away from Bronken, but couldn't.

The vider's surface temperature fell by the second, and Tessa's fingers started to ache. Veins of frost crept up the metal. She gripped it as best as she could, trying to ignore the satisfied smirk spreading across

Bronken's face. He seemed unaffected by the cold.

"I don't know if I can hold on much longer," she breathed to Gus. Tessa's fingers started to throb.

Then at her elbow, she heard Hodges. She suddenly remembered yelling at him and felt small. But he put his hand on her arm and kept singing to her. His voice sounded like a bright thread stitching a pattern into the rest of the music, and Tessa felt a prick of hope.

She looked up at Bronken. "You aren't going to get this!" she said, squeezing her almost-numb fingers as tightly as she could.

"Is that right?" his voice vibrated in her chest. "It looks like I already have."

"It's not yours!" Angry, scared tears burned Tessa's eyes. Her fingers were turning blue at the tips.

Even Gus was singing his heart out now. Every new voice made Tessa feel a little stronger. She gripped the vider harder, yelping at the pain. The cold felt like nails driving into her fingertips. She held on, screaming, as her legs buckled, and she fell hard on her knees.

Music and wind began to whip around her, blowing her hair. The Shellstalkers grew louder now, too, and she could hear snippets of their words …. *YOU'RE WEAK… STOP… YOU CAN'T… GIVE UP…* She wrenched her mind away from their voices and clung to the music in her ears. Her arm started shaking, and then her whole body as she fought to hold on.

The sky behind the Shellstalkers darkened, and icy wind hit Tessa's face, making even her lips feel numb. Lightning stabbed the sky, and thunder boomed.

Tessa closed her eyes to focus on the music, choking back sobs. She was losing her grip. "I'm so sorry!" she whimpered. The pain climbed up her arm.

The wind pushed so violently that even on her knees, Tessa had to fight to stay upright. Then Bronken began to laugh. It was a deep terrifying sound, and as he laughed, his body started to grow bigger in front of her. He grew, pulling Tessa up with him until she was standing again on weak trembling legs, looking up at his towering form. He laughed and laughed, the sound careening over the chaos.

The ground shuddered, and Tessa heard people scream. She turned her head in time to see the professor stumble and crash to the ground.

"Professor!" she yelled.

But he didn't get up. Only his mouth moved, still trying to sing, and then it stopped all together.

CHAPTER 39

"Professor!" Tessa felt her own voice stick in her throat as she stared up at Bronken, who now stood ten feet high with glee on his face. People kept screaming around her. *I'm fighting for their lives,* she told herself, and the professor's slack face flashed through her head. She jammed her whole palm against the vider. Pain drove through her shoulder into her chest.

Despite the fact that Tessa was literally freezing, sweat dripped down her face and mixed with her tears. "Help!" her voice cracked. She heard more Wholehearteds stumbling behind her. "Help!" she screamed.

"Hang on!!" someone yelled.

"They're falling!"

"Don't let go!"

"Hodges!" Gus's voice rose above the others'.

Hodges fell?! Tessa felt the sweat on her palms ice up against the metal. "Not Hodges," she whimpered. She couldn't feel her hand at all anymore.

"Fight, Tessa! You have to hold on!" Gus shouted. She clenched her eyes shut to focus all her energy on keeping the vider under her hand.

"Gloria!" someone yelled.

Calls for Gloria erupted all over the field.

The ground rumbled and lurched.

Gloria! Tessa's mind groped toward the name as pain flooded her head. She wouldn't last. She couldn't. Her body trembled violently. Then a woman's face filled her vision, deep coffee-colored skin, a mass of thick grey braids, and black eyes that looked straight into Tessa's.

Gloria! Tessa gasped.

"Tessa," Gloria's voice was gentle and commanding at once, and made everything else fall silent. A deep warmth flooded Tessa's body and for a second, she felt like she was floating.

Then Bronken's cruel laugh thundered through the quiet. A pain stabbed Tessa's chest, and everything went dark.

CHAPTER 40

Every part of Tessa hurt, and the whole right side of her body was throbbing. Slowly she pried her eyes open, and the world swam into focus. She was lying in the alley. *Where was the field? Bronken?* She tried to get up but couldn't even lift her head. Her eyes ached and fell shut again. *The vider!* Tessa could feel it's hard shape still in her hand. *Bronken hadn't gotten it!*

"Hodges!" It was Gus. She heard him moving around behind her. "You ok?"

"Can't see," said Hodges.

"You can't see? Anything?" Gus asked, alarmed. Tessa listened, wishing she could roll over and look at them, but try as she might, she couldn't even manage to crack her eyes open again.

"Just feel," Hodges said. "Tessa."

"Tessa!" Gus shouted. Footsteps hurried toward her. "Tessa?" Gus crouched next to her. "Can you hear me?... She's not moving!" he called. "But she has the vider!" His voice rippled with relief. Tessa heard Hodges slowly walk closer. "Her arm," Gus went on. "It's all swollen, and her hand—" His voice dropped off, and Tessa knew she must look as bad as she felt. She wanted to talk to them, ask questions, but she was trapped in her unmoving body.

"Can feel it," said Hodges. "Pain."

"Tessa, wake up." Her eyes refused even to flutter. She tried yelling, and her voice released the smallest sound.

"I think she can hear us!" Gus sounded hopeful.

She tried to groan again, but nothing came out.

"C'mon, Tessa," Gus said more urgently, touching her good arm.

"She may not wake for a while," said a soothing voice behind them.

"Michael!" Gus said. "What's happening? How did we get here? Hodges can't see! And look at Tessa." Tessa heard his voice catch.

"I know," Michael said. His voice sounded sad. "We took quite a hit. Tessa was a fighter, all right. Hodges, you're going to have to see with your heart for a while."

"They need help!" Gus sounded frantic.

"It will take time," Michael said. Tessa sensed Michael crouching down next to her. She felt like she'd been hit by a bus. Her head pounded, and her arms and legs felt broken, even her ribs hurt. Michael touched Tessa's hand and started to pull the vider from it. The metal stuck to her palm and fingers. Michael had to tug, and Tessa howled as he ripped it free. The sound came out as more of a moan, but Gus shrieked loudly, as if for her. Tessa could feel tears streaming from her closed eyes as her raw skin met the air.

"Sorry, Tessa," Michael said, resting his hand on her head for a moment. "You fought for this one. Let me clean it and then, Gus," Tessa could already hear Michael rubbing the vider on something, "you'd better hold on to it." Tessa's body begin to shake again.

"Should we call 911? Should I get my mom? What do we do?" Gus asked.

"First I think we need Hodges," Michael said.

"Hodges?" Gus asked weakly.

Hodges's small hand touched Tessa's shoulder and felt its way down her hot swollen arm to her hand. Even his gentle touch burned. Hodges carefully lifted

230

her singed hand and kissed each finger. The relief was instant. The pounding in her head and chest ceased, and the fiery pain in her arms and legs drained away. Tessa tried again to open her eyes. They fluttered for a second, just enough to glimpse Hodges's unseeing eyes and the small smile on his face. *Thank you,* she tried to say. *Thank you.* She hoped he could feel it.

"What?" Gus stammered. "Her — her skin! All the cuts are gone! It's not even red. Hodges! How'd you *do* that?" Gus's hand brushed Tessa's palm. "It's just scars now." His voice brimmed with wonder.

"Healing's a rare gift," said Michael.

"Can you do that to your eyes?" Gus asked Hodges.

"No," said Hodges. "Gloria."

Tessa heard a vibrating sound and knew Hodges's compass must be lighting up.

"Two hours, 14 minutes?!" Gus said, confirming her suspicion.

"This isn't over," Michael said.

"But —" Gus protested. "But we have the vider! They didn't get it!" His voice quieted. "We can't keep going."

"It feels that way," said Michael. "But time's nearly out, and no one is safe until the vider is back on The Great Invention. We must save the Era." There was a sound down the alley, and Tessa heard Michael stand up quickly. "Professor," he said in a low voice.

Gus gasped. "What happened to you?" He sounded horrified. "You're —"

"Transparent, yes," the professor finished. His voice sounded tired. "And this leg's gone all together." Tessa heard a tapping sound like a stick or cane against the ground. "This is the closest I've ever come to disappearing."

"But," Gus sounded like he was searching for words. "Tessa has the vider and —"

"And The Great Invention needs it," the professor finished.

"But will you—reappear? I mean, *can* you?"

"Everything depends on the restoration of The Great Invention," the professor said.

"But Tessa can't go," said Gus. "And Hodges is blind." His voice dropped. "I can't find it alone."

"You can," the professor said earnestly. "And Gus, you are not alone. We are never alone. The Unseen teaches us this. Tessa has battled, and it will take her body a while to restore itself. But she's getting stronger, even now. Don't lose hope." His voice, though weary, sounded encouraging. "Michael," he continued, "we must do what we can. Come."

"So many have fallen, Professor, but yes, we must try. Kids, be strong. You *are* strong," Michael said.

Tessa certainly didn't feel strong. Someone squeezed her hand encouragingly. Then she heard the professor's broken steps walking away.

CHAPTER 41

"They left," Gus said in a hollow voice. "What do we do?" His voice sounded muffled like he was covering his face.

"Piggyback?" Hodges asked.

"Really?" Gus gave a half-laugh. "Think it's ok to move her?" He paused for a second. "I guess I can try." Gus crouched down and pulled Tessa onto his back. She hung like a ragdoll.

Slowly Gus straightened and took a deep breath. "Hodges, can you hold onto my arm and walk? We have to get to Mom and Dad."

"And the lens," Hodges said as they began a slow walk out of the alley.

"I forgot about the lens," Gus said. "I guess we still need that."

Tessa's arms and legs dangled limply, and it felt funny not to be able to move them at all. After a few minutes, she heard Marcus.

"Gus! Is she ok?" Marcus helped Gus carry Tessa to the porch swing.

"And Hodges?" Mika said urgently.

"Can't see but ok," said Hodges.

"Can't see?!"

"It was a battle." Gus swallowed hard. "And the professor is half-disappeared. He said we still have to get to The Great Invention, and there are only two hours left." Tessa didn't like how deflated Gus sounded. Had he given up? She wished, again, she could talk.

"Adam's at the train station," Mika said urgently. "We can talk in the car." Gently Marcus lifted Tessa up again. She heard the van door open, and he laid her on the seat, pulling a seatbelt across her body.

Gus talked all the way to the station, describing every detail of the battle he could remember. Tessa learned that while she'd been fighting Bronken, Wholehearteds all around them had been fading and falling. Some had disappeared completely. *What if Hodges had? Or the professor?*

The van stopped, and Tessa's dad opened the door.

"To what do I owe this fanfare —" Adam's bright voice filled the car, then stopped suddenly. "What happened!" he climbed in next to Tessa and gently held her shoulders. "Is she all right?" he asked urgently.

"Dad!" she tried to yell, dying to throw her arms around him. Sound came out this time, but it sounded more like "Naaa."

"Tessa!"

She pried her eyes open and saw her dad's face for a brief second before they shut again.

"She opened her eyes!" Gus yelled.

"What's happened?" Adam asked again.

"A lot," Marcus said. "They have the Ultimate Vider."

"What?" Adam gasped. "What?!" He asked again, and Tessa realized she hadn't talked to him in days.

"She was in a battle," said Gus. "And she saved the Ultimate."

"How'd you get a vider? The *Ultimate?* How did this happen?"

"They got one the same way we did once," Mika answered. "From the professor."

"And we're almost out of time!" Gus said. "We need the lens on your keychain."

Tessa managed to open her eyes again, and this time they stayed open. She couldn't tell if the look on her dad's face was awe or horror. "My *lens?*" He fumbled in his pocket for his keys. "Wow, I've had this on my keyring so long I nearly forgot what it was." Tessa saw him glance at Mika as he handed his keys to Gus.

"Tess," he said turning back to her. "How in the world..." He ran his finger along her fresh scars. It didn't hurt at all. Tessa leaned forward and tried to sit up but the effort was exhausting, and she flopped her head back against the seat again.

"It's ok," her dad soothed. "Just rest." His eyes looked scared.

"We're using the lenses to find The Great Invention," Gus explained. Tessa heard the dread, and again tried to reassure him, but her voice came out like a moan.

The van pulled away from the curb.

"Where are we going?" Adam asked.

"We're not altogether sure. But I'll head in the direction of the professor's house while Gus looks," said Mika.

"Wow," Gus said, holding up Adam's lens, still connected to his keys. "It's just a smaller version of ours." Tessa watched Gus work the gold coin off of the keychain and measure it against the narrow end of the vider. "It fits perfectly," he said twisting it on. The vider looked strange now with both lenses covered by opaque coins, but Gus held it up to his eye anyway. Then he screamed.

CHAPTER 42

Mika swerved in surprise. "What's wrong?!"

"He's using the lenses," Adam clarified.

Gus was breathing hard, and fear lit his face. "It's everything at once," Gus said. "The clouds are full of Shellstalkers — their faces. They're all moving, and they look brutal!" He shuttered. "And there are creatures everywhere, and glowing people I couldn't see before. There are so many feelings. It's all shaking and full of light. It's too much."

Suddenly thunder cracked. Tessa's body flinched as she remembered the field. Wind pushed against the van. It sounded like they were driving through another battle.

"But I can also feel the singing," Gus went on. "In my chest like bass."

Tessa felt strength coming back into her body and tried to sit up again. This time her elbows held her.

"I can't look at the people!" Gus cringed and shoved the vider at Tessa's dad. "It's too much!"

"A door," Hodges said, reminding Gus what they were doing.

"I can't," Gus said. He glanced at Tessa and saw she was watching him, now. "It's so much stronger than before," he apologized.

"I taaaa," said Tessa. She'd meant to say, I'll try, but her mouth hadn't caught up with her brain yet. She laughed, but instead of a laugh, a snort came out, which made her snort again. Gus cracked a half-smile. At least she could move her mouth.

Tessa looked down at her hand with its long scars. It looked like someone else's hand. She touched the pink marks along each of her fingers, remembering the pain that had hurt into her bones. Cautiously she flexed her fingers. They were stiff but didn't hurt.

"This is why we have The Great Invention," Marcus said, reaching back to put his hand on Gus's knee. "It makes everything right — how much we see, and how much we don't have to see. We need that balance!"

Gus nodded. "Do you want to look?"

"I don't know if it'll work for me," Marcus said.

"But I'll try."

"Double lens," Mika said softly from the driver's seat. "Changes everything."

Marcus took the vider from Gus, and everyone waited. "Oh," Marcus inhaled sharply. "I'd forgotten." For a few moments he just stared, then, as if in shock, handed the vider back to Adam.

Adam took a big breath like he was about to dive under water, and then looked. He sat riveted, and Tessa saw him shiver slightly. "It *is* too much," he said, finally. "Mika, I think you're going the right way, though. There's lots of activity up ahead, even in the sky." He gave the vider back to Gus.

"Door, Gus," Hodges said.

Gus paused. "Ok. I'll look for one, but I'm *not* looking at the people." Tessa saw him brace himself and turn back to the window. "Packasindrias are surrounding the car!" he shouted excitedly. "They're running next to us. I think they're doing it on purpose. Their hair's blowing over the windows like a screen — Oh! Don't hit it!" Gus yelled.

Mika slammed on the breaks. "A Packasindria?"

"No, my eagle! It's right in front of the windshield!" Gus said. "He's massive!"

"A Soenta," Mika breathed. "They look like

enormous eagles."

A Soenta. Tessa tried out the word in her head. She craned her neck to see it but only saw a pigeon flapping in front of the car.

"Turn right here," Gus said. "I think we've got to follow it." Confidence built in his voice. Tessa remembered her dream at the pool, how a huge white bird had helped Gus. *Is this the same one?*

Mika slammed on the brakes. "Road Closed? Tell me where to go," she said backing the car into a three-point turn. "This guy won't get off my tail!" Mika glanced again in the rearview mirror and tapped the brakes. Tessa pulled on the back of the seat to help herself sit up taller and saw a black van practically against their bumper. She didn't recognize the driver but judging from his slick combed hair and smooth-shaven face, she had a guess.

"The Soenta's turning," Gus said, using the new word as if he'd always known it. "Go left here!"

Mika obeyed, and Tessa watched the driver behind them glare as he cut the wheel and followed. "Another detour?" Mika read the sign. "There's a water main break up ahead! What a mess! All these roads are closed!" She turned the van around again.

"There's a bunch of Shellstalkers over there," Gus

said, pointing to a group of people near the construction site. "And they look happy," he said with disgust.

A small pit of fear settled in Tessa's stomach for the first time since the battle.

"This whole section of the city is closed down! And I don't think it's a coincidence," Mika said.

"No, it's not," Gus agreed. "I think my Soenta's circling the water main break, past those barricades where the streets are closed."

The black van pulled to the curb behind them, and two tall men in crisp ironed shirts got out and jogged over to the crowd. The Shellstalkers weren't gathered in the construction site where Gus was pointing but were close enough to worry Tessa.

"I think I need to get out here, too," Gus said with dread in his voice. "I've got to follow the Soenta,"

Mika glanced nervously out the window as Gus opened the sliding door and climbed out. Tessa swung her legs off the seat, too, and started to stand up.

"You can't come, can you?" Gus asked doubtfully.

"I haavoooo —" Still no clear words, but Tessa already felt much more like herself, and her legs held her up. She nodded.

Gus looked at his parents uncertainly, but no one argued. "You need to look with this first," he said, handing the vider to Tessa. "Prepare yourself."

Tessa nodded. But nothing could have prepared her for what she saw through the vider: The sky teamed with low swooping birds, and bodies with cruel angry faces appeared and disappeared in the clouds. The street was crowded, normal for rush hour, but Tessa could feel the piercing intensity of each person's feelings. The reds and browns of a man pacing at the traffic light shot through Tessa like fire, and she felt his rage consume her. Her scarred hand throbbed, and fear dropped like an anchor in her stomach. "I can't do this," she said, flinging down the vider, startled to hear her mouth working. "I don't want to go," she said again.

"I don't either," said Gus. "But we have to — for Hodges and the professor. You didn't see him but — he's almost gone."

Tessa squeezed her eyes shut as if she could disappear. All she could think of was Bronken's jeering face and the pain shooting up her arm. *I can't go*, she thought. *I can't.* Hodges moved to stand next to her and leaned against her arm. Suddenly, Gloria's face burst into Tessa's mind. Tessa saw Gloria's deep eyes looking steadily at her and felt a small surge of strength. *Fear has no place here.* Gloria's voice was deep and certain. It echoed through Tessa's thoughts and when it quieted, Gloria was gone. And so was Tessa's dread. Tessa opened her eyes, taking a deep breath. "Ok," she said. "Let's go."

"You sure?" Gus asked, relieved.

She nodded, afraid her voice would crack if she spoke again.

"We'll come, too," Tessa's dad said eagerly.

Tessa imagined facing the Shellstalkers with Mika, Marcus, and her dad, and her heart jumped. *That would change everything!*

"We want to come with you, but we can't," Marcus said gently, glancing at Adam.

"Of course." Adam's face fell. "We can't get into the Unseen, anymore. I got swept up in the moment." He smiled apologetically at Tessa and squeezed her. "This is your time. You've got this."

"And you're not alone. I know that," Mika said. Her eyes looked sad but her voice was strong. "We'll be right here. And we'll be singing."

The kids hugged and kissed the parents, and Tessa noticed Mika gripping Marcus's hand. As Tessa, Gus, and Hodges walked away, their parents burst into song, and the music felt almost like they were walking together.

CHAPTER 43

"One of us will have to use the vider and lead the others," Gus said with forced confidence as they walked.

"I can." Tessa's voice wobbled as the Shellstalker sky flashed back in her head.

"No, me," Hodges said. They looked down at his little round face.

"But you can't see?" Gus said, stating the obvious. Hodges looked unafraid and without further argument, Gus plunked the vider into his hand.

Hodges took Tessa's hand, and she linked arms with Gus to avoid hurting his broken fingers. When all three of them were connected, Hodges looked through the vider. As soon as he did, Tessa and Gus began to see, too, but not all at once like when they'd found the doorframe. This time the buildings began to shimmer and lose their sense of permanence. Bright sky suddenly glowed through the storm clouds, and though they couldn't make out   Shellstalkers' faces, they noticed dark shadows diving in the clouds.

The group of Shellstalkers gathered up ahead softened into a smoky cloud, and Tessa took a deep breath. "Just smoke," she said, following Hodges. As they walked, the sidewalk felt softer underfoot, and she saw glimmers of green breaking through the pavement. Like Gus had described, Tessa could feel the singing somehow deep in her chest, and it made her feel stronger.

Hodges led on. With each step, Tessa could see more of the Unseen world. She caught glimpses of white animals out of the corners of her eyes, but when she turned to see them straight on, they vanished. The animals, Tessa somehow knew, were escorting them.

"Can you see that?" Gus asked, squinting at a white sheen hovering in front of them.

"There's something there," said Tessa. "It's staying with us."

"I think that's my eagle," Gus said.

Tessa looked harder. She couldn't make out wings, but a bright shape blocked some of the dark swirling sky. She kept her eyes fixed on the blur. It was definitely leading them.

The city noise was growing — a jackhammer started, grunting trucks, blaring horns, traffic — and the scenery became a jumble of worlds crashed together. Tessa couldn't make sense of where they were going.

"Hodges, what do you see? Are we close?"

Hodges kept pulling them along. He held up the compass, vibrating and searing-white now.

"18 Minutes!" Gus read aloud, exchanging glances with Tessa.

"Michael," Hodges said.

In the bustle of people with briefcases and take-out bags, Tessa saw Michael. "Up ahead!" Tessa yelled excitedly. He seemed simultaneously to be wearing his dirty green t-shirt and his white combat boots. The more they focused on him, the more his glowing fatigues emerged.

Michael motioned to them and started running. The three kids followed. They felt clumsy, bumping into each other as they hurried, still linked together, but they held on. Hodges huffed as they rushed down the sidewalk, and Tessa wondered if he could intensely feel all the people's emotions they passed, but it was too hard to ask.

In the midst of the glittering grasses and dirty streets, a steady drumming started, far off but growing louder. It was the most complicated rhythm Tessa had ever heard; it made her want to move and dance. She was just beginning to jump when Hodges screeched to a halt. She slammed into his back and bumped her chin hard against his head.

"Ow!" Tessa rubbed her face. "Hodges, are you ok?" They all let go, and instantly the Unseen world — glowing Michael, drumming, and the shimmering green — vanished, leaving them in the blaring chaos of rush hour in a construction zone.

CHAPTER 44

"Yeah," Hodges groaned, holding the back of his head.

"Sorry!" Tessa said. She followed Hodges across the street. Orange lights flashed along the top of the construction barricade, and a big yellow bulldozer grunted in front of them.

"Where did Michael go?" Tessa asked.

"Don't know," said Hodges, still breathing hard. He was holding the vider up to his blind eyes and pointed it at the clustered hive of machinery in the middle of the construction site. "The Great Invention," he said.

Tessa strained to see past the obvious. *Was he serious? Could The Great Invention really be here, of all places?*

Hodges took their hands again, and the Unseen flashed back into view: about 50 yards in front of them, where a crane, cement mixer, and cluster of yellow machines had just stood was now an intricately carved stone and wood building, flecked with color. It had to be The Great Invention.

"It's kind of blurry," Tessa said, squinting.

"For me, too," said Gus.

"Archway." Hodges tugged them toward a free-standing wooden arch that Tessa couldn't believe she hadn't noticed. Designs were carved into every inch of it — many-petaled flowers, birds with perfect feathers, chipmunks, leafy vines. Tessa ran her fingers along the handiwork, mesmerized, until Hodges gave a sharp tug and pulled her through.

Immediately, the world altered. The dim evening and grimy city vanished completely into a sparkling bright meadow surrounded by massive trees. The Invention, itself, stood in perfect focus now, and Tessa took off running toward it.

It was so much more beautiful than she had imagined. The Great Invention was made entirely from the earth — some pillars were huge tree trunks with the bark still on them, others had playful patterns carved deep into the wood. Archways, like the one they'd just walked through, were cut into the thick walls and framed large sparkling windows. Spears of quartz and agate dazzled the walls and cast shimmering reflections on the ground as the light hit them. It was breathtaking. Tessa could hear the drumming and chimes, the beautiful music pouring out of The Great Invention, but the sounds were noticeably slowing down.

Hodges yelped, and Tessa saw him fling the compass to the ground. It was red and flashing now and looked like it was smoking. Gus leaned over it. "One minute and 30 seconds?! We're here, but where do we put the vider?"

Tessa ran toward The Great Invention. The walls towered above her, and though there were archways and windows, she couldn't find a door. There had to be a way in! She frantically pushed against everything she could and ran her hands along the wall looking for a handle or knob or anything that would open. Gus did the same as The Great Invention groaned and creaked even more. The music had almost stopped. "How do we get in!" Tessa's heart pounded.

Hodges stumbled and sank to the ground.

"No!" Gus ran to him. Hodges's body started to blink in and out of focus as though his existence, itself, were flickering. *The End of the Era* — the words rang through Tessa's head as she watched Hodges struggle. *It can't be!* Hodges, the professor, Mika, and her mom flashed through her head. *I have to get in!*

Suddenly Allergia and a crowd of Shellstalkers materialized at the edge of the trees. They were still a ways off but were moving in like a wave. Tessa's scarred hand started to pound. She felt paralyzed as she watched their glaring faces come closer.

Tessa glanced at Hodges slumped in the grass and with alarm, realized the Invention was hardly making any sound. *Was its power so weak now that the Shellstalkers could come close to it?* Her heart pounded.

"We've given you several chances," said Allergia. "Now we're taking what we want." Her claw-like hands flexed at her sides.

A burning feeling climbed up Tessa's arm, and the skin of her hand turned red before her eyes. Gus was still kneeling in the grass holding his brother when the compass suddenly buzzed, flashed, and went dark.

Even from where she stood, Tessa could read the single glinting image: **0**.

They were out of time.

Bronken's laughter broke the silence like thunder. "HAHAHA!" he crowed. Lightning cut the sky. He was only an arm's length away now.

"Poor girl," Bronken said, reaching for Tessa's face.

The graze of his fingers broke her spell.

"Don't touch me!" Tessa screamed, jerking her face away, and Gloria's words shot through her: *Fear has no place here.* Bronken stumbled as if he'd been pushed. "This isn't over yet!" Tessa yelled.

Wind kicked up, and Tessa started screaming. A wordless battle cry unleashed from deep inside of her. As she yelled, a wobbly barrier, like the skin of a bubble, formed between her and the Shellstalkers. Fury poured out of her, and the more she screamed, the more the bubble swelled, pushing the Shellstalkers back until they stood ten feet away. "Gus! Find a way in!"

He hesitated only for a second, then lowered Hodges to the ground and ran to the Invention. Tessa glanced over to see him pounding on a spongy green moss wall that looked like it could be a doorway. But it wasn't opening. When she looked back, the Shellstalkers had pushed closer again.

Fear washed through her. Tessa started to chant and yell, but the barrier wasn't holding. The Shellstalkers' faces were moving in slow motion toward her.

"I'm trying to find a way in!" Gus banged and pressed frantically. "I can't *open* it!" he yelled in frustration.

Tessa didn't dare take her eyes off the Shellstalkers again. She wasn't sure how much longer she could hold them back. They were pressing against the barrier. "Hurry! Hurry!" she urged Gus. Bronken's outstretched arm came nearer by the second. His grabbing fingers were now only inches from Tessa.

"Help!" Tessa screamed "Gloria!"

CHAPTER 45

A deafening crack split the air, and Gloria filled the entire clearing, her grey hair falling in thick braids, woven with flowers and jewels. Her eyes shone like suns as they swept over the crowd.

Tessa felt both the impulse to fling herself at Gloria and to curl up in a ball and hide.

Gloria's eyes cut to the Shellstalkers. "Enough!" she roared. At her words, the Shellstalkers flew backwards and slammed against the trees with such force that Tessa shrieked. Instantly they exploded into clouds of black ash.

Silence fell.

The Invention had stopped its syncopated rhythms and now hoarsely creaked a single note. Tessa held her breath waiting for another sound, an assurance that it was, indeed, still working, but no other sounds came. She bit the inside of her cheek to steady herself, and her body trembled.

"We didn't make it," Gus whispered, looking back at Hodges's unmoving body.

"Gus." Gloria's voice was soft and firm at once like a velvet couch. He looked up. "Gus," she said again, her eyes on him.

"I couldn't find a way in," he croaked, and Tessa noticed tears smeared on his cheeks.

"We were so close," Tessa said. Her stomach churned, and she felt sick. "We ran out of time." She stared at the ground, then stooped and picked up the dull compass from the grass. It wasn't hot anymore.

"Ahh yes, time. I gave you time to help you move forward," Gloria said, "to bring you here with haste." As Gloria walked closer, she seemed less huge, but even more powerful. Tessa involuntarily stepped backward. "But time," Gloria continued, "is how *you* think; it's how *your* world works. I have no need for it. I exist at all times and can see all things at once."

Tessa's tired brain strained to understand.

"I'd already seen you arrive," Gloria continued. "But *you* needed to know you would, so I gave you time, like an arrow to follow." She looked at them intently.

Tessa thought of the blue arrows in the alley and wondered, briefly, if Gus was thinking of them, too. "So, the time didn't matter?" Tessa asked, doubtfully.

"It mattered," Gloria said. "Time constricts and orders your lives — you needed it to fight against. Time creates meaning."

"But —" said Gus weakly, dropping to his knees beside Hodges's pale body.

"*But,*" continued Gloria, "time isn't everything."

Tessa looked up at the towering mysterious machine that now stood perfectly still. Her voice felt buried deep inside, and when she spoke it hardly came out. "We didn't get here in time…The Invention stopped," she said.

"Child," Gloria said walking toward The Great Invention. Beside the mossy wall Gus had banged on, a Red Bud tree grew, heavy with dark pink blossoms. Gloria put her hand on the smooth stone behind it. Tessa now saw the wall was white and flecked with fiery colors. *Opal?* she wondered, suddenly thinking of the birthstone her mom always wore. Gloria flashed her a knowing smile, and Tessa turned to see if Gus had noticed, but he was still in the grass, bent over Hodges, who looked sickly translucent now. "Oh,"

Tessa said quietly, her heart plummeting.

"You could have helped him!" Gus burst out, looking up at Gloria. "Why didn't you?" His eyes shone with tears.

Gloria didn't say anything but walked over to Gus. She lay her hand on the top of his head. Gus looked up and opened his mouth to protest, but Gloria held his eye and spoke too softly for Tessa to hear. Gus looked angry and sad as he listened. But after a few seconds, he hugged Hodges, wiped his face with his hand, and stood up.

"Now," Gloria said, giving Gus a gentle nod, "you have something left to do." She walked back toward the Red Bud tree, put her palm on the white wall again, and then pressed. Tessa gasped as a section of the wall slid over to reveal an old-fashioned keyhole, the size of Tessa's hand, cut into the stone.

"We have to *unlock* that?" Tessa asked in surprise.

"The key would have to be huge," Gus said.

Tessa glanced over at Hodges and wondered if the professor were disappearing right now, too. *What does Gloria expect us to do?* she wondered, fidgeting uncomfortably. *We're out of time!* Gus's brow was furrowed, and he was staring at the keyhole with concentration.

"Could…we…" Gus began. Tessa could tell from his tone that he was working on a puzzle — he always talked ridiculously slowly whenever he puzzled. *But we have to hurry,* Tessa thought, squeezing her hands together. Gus frowned at the keyhole, studying the shape. Tessa squinted at it, too. *Why aren't we looking for a key?*

Suddenly Gus exploded, "I see it! It's how they fit together!" Tessa watched, bewildered, as Gus took the Ultimate Vider and compass from her and hurried toward the wall. The compass began to glow softly.

Gus held the vider with the wide end pointing down, and then held the compass up like a clock so Tessa could see its glowing face. As soon as he touched the compass's metal rim to the small end of the vider, they stuck together. "They're magnetic!" Gus shouted. "And really strong. I can't pull them apart again!"

"The puzzle!" said Gloria proudly, and Tessa remembered the story of their parents working to separate the pieces so many years ago.

Tessa now saw that the objects — the round compass on top, and the vider, wide-end down — created a keyhole-shaped sculpture that Gus was already lining up with the cut-out in the wall. He carefully inserted it into place. The vider-and-compass key fit perfectly.

Percussive music, bells, and drumming broke the tense silence, and the Unseen world surged into view.

Tessa caught a movement out of the corner of her eye and squealed as she saw Hodges tug the back of Gus's shirt.

Gus whirled around. "Hodges! You're alive!" Gus grabbed his brother in a tight squeeze. "Are you ok? Can you see?" He pulled back to look at him as Hodges nodded and smiled shyly at Gloria.

At once Tessa could see Gus's blue and green currents swirling, and Hodges's glowy marshmallow interior. Their actual bodies seemed to change, too. Gus looked suddenly older, and he filled out his broad shoulders. Tessa was sure he stood taller, and his laugh sounded weightier. Hodges immediately plunked himself down in the grass next to some Packasindrias. He still looked like a little kid, but he seemed different. Tessa couldn't put her finger on why until she realized he was chatting away — chatting! — telling the animals a story.

"All is restored!" Gloria sang. "And you now have a glimpse of how *I* see you." Tessa looked again at their dancing colors and vibrant faces, and when she looked down at herself, she could even see her own pink and gold licking flames. She wished she could see like this all the time.

"It would be too much," Gloria warned, answering the words Tessa hadn't spoken. "But you already know that."

Bright white creatures appeared everywhere — wispy Packasindrias and elephant-like Treetos, wide-winged eagles, and dozens of animals they'd never seen before. Birds soared through the air, and for a brief moment, a huge white eagle landed on Gus's shoulder, causing him to stumble slightly before he stood up straight to hold it. The bird seemed to lean against him for a moment, and then took flight, soaring into the sky. Thousands of Wholehearteds poured into the field. They wore sparkling white clothing and sang. Tessa stood, spellbound: looking, breathing, listening. The Wholehearteds were safe!

Then Michael and the professor emerged from the crowd. The professor's body was solid again, and he walked easily on his now-healthy legs, almost skipping as he neared them. His insides popped with flaring rockets and firework explosions, and Tessa marveled that she'd never thought to look at him through the vider before.

"The Great Invention!" the professor cheered.

"Heart-Sight lives on!" Michael echoed, and his fatigues glowed more brilliantly than ever. "Those Shellstalkers will finally quiet down now that the balance is restored!" They all hugged each other at once.

"That wasn't easy, was it?" the professor said. "I sure am glad to have this back!" He patted the leg that had disappeared and laughed a hearty laugh. "You didn't give up," he said, suddenly serious, looking at the three of them intently.

Tessa felt her face flush, and she looked down at her shoes.

"No, Tessa," the professor continued. "Questioning — even doubting — is not the same as giving up. Some of us must wrestle for our belief more than others. I dare say, you wrestled, and I think you found it." His eyes twinkled, and Tessa smiled gratefully at him.

"No one can see quite the same way after using a vider," the professor continued. "Especially the Ultimate. Once you've seen inside people, you can't help but notice there's more than meets the eye. Even without a vider. Wait and see for yourself."

"Hey! What about this?" Gus asked, pulling his parents' old vider from his pocket.

"Oh, keep that as a souvenier!" the professor

chortled. "And you never know. Maybe one day it will show you a door again, for a purpose we can't yet imagine!" The professor smiled his crooked smile, and Gus grinned, shoving the vider back into his pocket.

"You must come visit soon!" the professor insisted, hugging them goodbye for now. "We'll have tea." He winked at Tessa.

"I'll eat at your house any day!"

Then Gloria called to the kids. She held her arms open wide and easily scooped all three of them into a hug. Every good smell Tessa had ever known seemed to come from Gloria's skin, and she leaned in. Before Gloria let them go, she kissed each of their heads. "Now," she said with excitement in her voice, "there are people waiting for you."

CHAPTER 46

A plain wooden door with a brass knob appeared at the edge of the clearing and slowly opened. Through it, the children could see Mika, Marcus, and Adam in the professor's breakfast nook, looking around eagerly.

"They can't see you yet," Gloria said. "They can only hear the music and feel the goodness. Go on." She looked kindly at each of them. "You have much to catch up on!"

As badly as Tessa wanted to run to her dad, she felt a pang of reluctance and stared at Gloria's beautiful face, the woman who somehow could fill the whole field and whisper right in Tessa's ear at the same time. Tessa studied each jewel and flower braided into her hair, the deep brown eyes, the layers of fabric that looked both weighty and weightless at once, and promised herself never to forget a single detail. *Will I ever see her again?* Tessa wondered.

"Child, don't worry," Gloria said, once again answering Tessa's unspoken question. "Once you've found me, you never leave me. Your mama knew that, too." Suddenly an image of Tessa's mom glimmered beside Gloria. As it grew solid, Tessa could see both her mom and brilliant pink light dancing inside of her. Her mom swept her into a hug and squeezed with as much strength and love as always. Then she looked right at Tessa with big teary eyes, smiled, and kissed her on the face. "I love you, Tessa!"

"I love you, Mom." Tessa choked the words out, staring in disbelief at her mom's face, right in front of her.

Her mom hugged her again, long and hard. "I wish we could stay just like this," her mom said. Tessa inhaled. Her mom smelled like she always had, of fresh laundry and peppermint gum. "But, my girl, home is waiting for you." Her voice had a smile in it. "So much is waiting for you!" She pulled back so they were nose to nose. "I'm so, so proud of you, Tess."

"Don't go!" Tessa couldn't help but cry as her mom squeezed her hands and began to shimmer and disappear from sight. "I love you!" Her mom sang out as she went. "I love you!" and her pink light hung in the air for a moment.

"I love *you*!" Tessa cried. Gloria's arms were around her now as the tears poured down Tessa's face. Gloria let her cry hard right into her dress, without a care for the beautiful fabrics of shimmering light. Then after a few minutes, very gently, Gloria said, "Your mom is right, Tessa. Though she can't stay with you, you have that." Gloria gestured toward the door.

The boys were already tearing across the field. Tessa took a huge breath and wiped her eyes with the back of her hand. "Ok," she nodded at Gloria's reassuring face. She took one final look around at the rich blue sky streaked with golden-pinks. She couldn't help but glance again at the space where her mom had stood, but it was empty now. Through the doorway, she could see her dad looking for her, craning his neck to see around Mika and Marcus. Tessa met Gloria's eyes one last time and then began to run.

✳ ✳ ✳

As soon as Tessa burst through the door, her dad swept her into a hug. She felt other arms, too.

"Tess!" the arms squeezed.

"Molly?!" Tessa squealed. "You're here?" Seeing her sister in front of her almost felt like her mom's hug again.

"I came a little early after talking to this guy," she said, nodding toward their dad.

"He told you —" Understanding crashed over Tessa. "You already knew about the Unseen, didn't you?!" Tessa felt light-headed, and Molly squeezed her harder. Then everyone began talking and hugging at the same time.

"You did it!" Mika squealed, and Marcus laughed out loud.

"We did!" Tessa beamed at Gus. "I thought we were definitely lost when the Shellstalkers came back. My whole arm turned bright red!" Tessa stretched her hand out, remembering the burning. "But I guess it's ok now."

"And Hodges!" Gus almost shouted, whipping around to his brother. "You've got to stop collapsing and almost-dying! It's too stressful!" Hodges smiled bashfully, and Gus couldn't help but laugh with relief.

Then Tessa noticed the tray in the middle of the table piled with thick turkey sandwiches, watermelon, and icy glasses of lemonade. "Food!"

"Yeah, I'm starving!" Gus agreed. Everyone passed

plates around recounting the adventure.

"The Great Invention was so much more beautiful than I'd imagined!" Tessa said. "I wish we could have explored it for days. I bet it has so many secrets."

"Yeah, like the keyhole!" Gus agreed.

"I've only ever heard of it," said Molly.

"Same with us," said Mika nodding. "We've never seen it. I want to hear all the details!"

"Really?" Tessa couldn't believe it. "I figured every-one in the Unseen visits it."

"Not at all," said Marcus. "It's rare."

Tessa pictured The Invention in her head again and imagined the swirling, drumming, dancing sounds as Gus started sketching a picture on the checkered paper placemat in front of him. Along with the food, the professor had left a cup of pencils sitting on the table. How did he always know what they'd need? Gus drew the spiraled beams and arches, the glinting stones, and hefty tree-like pillars. He was just coloring the dark keyhole in the wall when he stopped and looked up at his parents. "You guys had a key, didn't you?"

"What do you mean?" Tessa asked.

"They had a vider, a compass, and a lens that all attached," he explained to Tessa. "The professor didn't just give you a puzzle," he said turning back to his parents. "He gave you a key, didn't he?"

"You've always been a good puzzle-solver," Marcus said, grinning.

"Woah." In all the recounting, their parents' vider hadn't even crossed Tessa's mind.

"But it wouldn't have been a key to The Great Invention," Gus continued, "since you just said you've never been there, and you didn't have the Ultimate. So what did it go to?" His eyes shone eagerly.

Tessa turned to her dad. "*Did* you have a key?"

"Looks like it's time for a story," Adam said, clapping his hands.

Tessa leaned over to Molly and whispered, "Do you know this story?"

Molly nodded. "You won't believe it."

The walls of the professor's house had green jungle print wallpaper today and the cushions were orange and shaped like animals. Tessa mindlessly picked up an elephant pillow and held it on her lap as she leaned back.

"You're right. We did have a key," Marcus said, "but it was a little different. We had to use ours to lock something up."

"Lock something *up*?" Gus asked.

"Well — some*one.*"

Gus's eyebrows shot up in surprise. "You locked someone up! With a vider key? Was it a Shellstalker?"

"Let's just say Bronken wasn't always the most powerful Shellstalker," Adam chimed in.

"But I thought he's been around forever!" Tessa interrupted.

"He has," said Mika. "But so has Rowah."

"*Rowah?*" Tessa's mouth fell open. "Rowah the friend you loved?!"

"Was a Shellstalker?" Gus finished.

"Sure was," Adam nodded.

"Want another?" Mika said, handing Gus the stack of quarter-cut sandwiches. "And we'll get the story going."

Tessa leaned against her dad's arm. He felt warm and solid. She looked around the table at all the faces. It wasn't exactly the family she'd thought she'd have, but it was most definitely a family. Tessa watched Gus angle an enormous piece of sandwich into his mouth. He caught her eye and tried not to spit crumbs across the table as he laughed. For the second time this afternoon, Tessa tried to memorize the moment: Gus being Gus, Molly home, Hodges nearly hidden behind a pile of watermelon rinds, and all of them safe around the professor's kitchen table.

Turning toward her sister, Tessa realized she hadn't had the chance to see what Molly or her dad looked like through the vider.

As Marcus began the story, Tessa studied Molly next to her and found she could easily envision Molly full of little flickering yellow flags. As she watched her dad's animated eyes, she pictured fresh cut wood, stacked in the sunshine, and could almost smell the sweet scent of it. Maybe she *was* going to see a little differently now.

Tessa turned her attention back to the table, and her heart jumped. Out of the corner of her eye, she saw a shimmer of pink at the table. It flashed and was gone. Unable to keep from smiling, Tessa settled back to hear her parents' story of their adventure with the vider.

THE END

Acknowledgements

First, special thanks to Silas, who survived the drudgery of handwriting camp. Without those dreaded drives, this book wouldn't have been born. Thanks for journeying through stories with me for years and years.

Eden, you are a master brainstormer! Thanks for listening, asking, catching tiny details, and cheering me on. You helped me walk this story through many middle years.

Maeve, I loved landing this plane with you as my co-pilot. Your enthusiasm feels like springtime.

Ben, you've built me a writing nook in every house, and you always believe more is possible. Thanks for the life support and wild cheering (and patience!) as I've finished this. I love you.

Thanks to my brother Max, faithful writing buddy, encourager, emergency reader/editor/designer. Ping!
To my brother Eli, a tireless believer in my creativity. Thanks for seeing me, and for editing, reading and all.
Thanks to my sister Kaia Joye for being in my corner, always. Thanks to my Mom, for marveling at and delighting in my creative pursuits. And to my Dad, for

letting me take him on his first journey into a magical world! (and for killer proofreading).

Thanks to dear friends who have held me, and my words, up through the years: Annemarie Mott Ewing, Sara Moyer (and reader Harper-Lou!), Kelly Callaghan (and reader Declan!), Lindsay Thorburn, Carrie Paschall, Mandy Ream (eyes peeled for her new book!) Lara Mellema, Emily McClain, Elizabeth Boocks, Annette Richards, Tiffany and Chris Himes, Hollie Moyer, Erin Clifford, Leslie Vance, Cary Umhau, Shannon Golub, Emily Schultz, Wanda Jones Yeatman, Peter Butter, and all the Newcotts.

Thanks to nieces and nephews galore — I love seeing you all become in the world: Emma, Madison, Olivia, Maxfield, Hudson, and Mirabella Himes; Amber, Mason, Miles, Calvin, and Anabel Newcott; Ella, Finn, Harper, and Mille Moyer; Jeshurun, Ryken, Aurora, Arthur, and Elodie Moyer; Juna and Wyeth Wesolowski; Shiloh and Asher Newcott; and honorary Madeleine, Claire, and Eliza Ewing. Love you.

Thanks to those who ignited this writing journey along the way: Ben Hatke, Heather Buchta, Marc Tyler Nobleman, Christine Henderson. Thanks to the many storytellers who remind me the world sparkles with magic, even now. And to the SCBWI community that inspires and also sometimes blows bubbles.

Thanks to Chris Sowers, my book designer, for all his time and patience in wrestling this book into shape; and many thanks to my illustrator Marco Marella who made my dreams into pictures.

And, finally, thanks to YOU who read this book! So glad you're out there. May we always strive to see the Unseen.

BRONWEN BUTTER NEWCOTT

Bronwen Butter Newcott grew up in Washington, DC where she loved finding sugar maple leaves, trash treasures and neighborhood cats. She earned her MFA in poetry at the University of Maryland and has had poems published in many journals. As well as raising three fun kids, she has taught high school English, led poetry groups for homeless writers, and co-run a local art studio. These days she spends time writing and teaching workshops in Southern California where she lives with her husband, three kids, and dog Pippin Longstocking.

@bronwenbutternewcott
racetothegreatinvention.com
linktr.ee/bronwenbutternewcott